INTO THE ASHES

WARRIORS OF THE FIANNA
BOOK THREE

BY
SOPHIA NYE

Text by Sophia Nye
Cover by Dar Albert

Dragonblade Publishing, Inc. is an imprint of Kathryn Le Veque Novels, Inc.
P.O. Box 23
Moreno Valley, CA 92556
ceo@dragonbladepublishing.com

Produced in the United States of America

First Edition June 2024
Trade Paperback Edition

ARE YOU SIGNED UP FOR DRAGONBLADE'S BLOG?

You'll get the latest news and information on exclusive giveaways, exclusive excerpts, coming releases, sales, free books, cover reveals and more.

Check out our complete list of authors, too!

No spam, no junk. That's a promise!

Sign Up Here

www.dragonbladepublishing.com

Dearest Reader;

Thank you for your support of a small press. At Dragonblade Publishing, we strive to bring you the highest quality Historical Romance from some of the best authors in the business. Without your support, there is no 'us', so we sincerely hope you adore these stories and find some new favorite authors along the way.

Happy Reading!

CEO, Dragonblade Publishing

Additional Dragonblade books by Author Sophia Nye

Warriors of the Fianna Series
Song of the Fianna (Book 1)
Prince of Fire (Book 2)
Into the Ashes (Book 3)

Also from Sophia Nye
Outlawed (Novella)

THE WARRIORS OF THE FIANNA

Deep in the heart of the Kingdom of Munster, the legendary King Brian Boru has brought an ancient brotherhood back to life: The Fianna. Now entering his senescence, King Brian has all but achieved his dream of becoming High King of Éire, uniting the nine kingdoms to defend Éire's emerald shores from *Fin Gall* raiders. He will need the aid of the kingdom's best warriors to complete his vision and claim the seat of the High King.

But it is no simple task to become a warrior of the Fianna. Seven trials, the same seven used by the ancient Fianna, test the mettle of all who would claim such an honor.

Intelligence: Memorize the twelve books of poetry, so that you may be knowledgeable on the history, genealogy, and legends of your people.

Defense: With naught but staff and shield, defend yourself from nine men's spears while standing deep in a hole.

Speed: Outrun pursuers through a forest, without being injured. But take care! Not a branch may be broken to prove your skill.

Movement: Leap over a tree with a height to match your own, then crawl beneath a branch lower than your knee.

Recovery: Run through the forest with all speed until you step upon a thorn. Remove it without slowing down!

Bravery: Fight outnumbered without faltering.

Chivalry: Marry for love.

Truth in our hearts,
Strength in our arms,
Honesty in our speech.

CHAPTER ONE

Ulaid, Éire
November, AD 1000

DIARMID RECLINED AGAINST the fallen trunk of an ancient oak, laughing as his companions dined by his side on day-old oatcakes—a brief respite from days of overland pursuit before the Fianna went to battle once more. This time, they pursued Aodh, King of Ailech, who had captured Princess Cara of Thurles. They intended to remedy that shortly.

These men, King Brian's Fianna warriors, had become Diarmid's family over the past year. He had trained, fought, and bled beside them. Even a few hours before a battle, nothing raised his spirits like moments shared with his fellow Fianna. Only a mug of ale and a woman in his lap could improve upon the evening. And though there was a woman present, she currently sat on Dallan's lap.

"You still haven't told us how you're here instead of in Laigin," Diarmid observed. "I thought your uncle wished you to leave the Fianna, yet here you are, traveling north alongside us with your lovely bride." He smiled at her warmly with his compliment.

Dallan glared daggers at him, nose flaring, as though Diarmid would *actually* attempt to steal his friend's lover. Honestly, he should be insulted.

"Well?" Finn, a warrior who could play the harp so well he could make a grown man weep, prodded Dallan. Of all of them,

Finn was both the tallest and fairest in coloring.

Dallan's lips tightened as he exchanged a look with Niamh, the golden-haired beauty on his lap. "It went poorly."

Every one of them knew what that meant.

"Which one of them tried to kill you?" Diarmid asked.

Niamh's bright blue eyes went wide. "How'd you know?"

"When things don't go our way, there's usually a sword involved, dear," Diarmid answered.

"She's not your dear," Dallan growled.

"I call every woman 'dear,'" Diarmid explained slowly, as though Dallan were addled.

Finn didn't even attempt to suppress a chuckle at Dallan's posturing. Diarmid's brother Conan joined right in with him.

Dallan frowned at them. "Laugh all you want. When it's your woman he's after, *I'll* be the one cackling."

"Now wait just a moment," Diarmid interrupted. "Never in my life have I stolen a woman from a friend."

"Come, now, Diarmid, you can hardly blame him," Finn replied smoothly. "In the ancient tales, was it not your namesake who stole Gráinne from Finn mac Cumhail?"

Diarmid narrowed his eyes at Finn. "Aye," he allowed. "And Finn mac Cumhail's first wife was turned into a deer. It seems to me he has trouble with wives, not friends."

"You bedded Ailis," his brother Conan accused. "Remember?" Conan turned to Finn and Dallan. "Love of my life, she was."

"She stole your jeweled dagger!" Diarmid wished his brother sat close enough to have his head smacked—maybe it would revive his memory.

Conan, his deep brown eyes the same as Diarmid's, had the gall to look affronted. "Then why did you bed her?"

"Oh, for the love of—"

"He hasn't gone two days without a woman warming his bed," Cormac, his eldest brother, muttered unhelpfully. In Diarmid's estimation, Cormac's manner of socializing was to sit, silently observing conversation, until he decided how he could best thwart it.

"That can't be true," Niamh countered, coming to his defense as she wrapped her arm about Dallan's shoulders. "Has he not been traveling nearly a sennight?"

Every one of his friends looked to him, their gazes filled with accusation.

"There was that farmer's daughter just north of Thurles," Finn offered.

"And the miller's daughter the day after," Conan added.

Illadan, who had ignored the conversation entirely as he stood guard, turned around. "Don't forget that widow."

"I'm glad to see my love life holds such interest for you all that you keep a running record."

"Who did he bed last night?" Dallan asked everyone except Diarmid.

"Tuala," Diarmid supplied quietly, smiling to himself as he recalled the lively evening.

"I'm impressed that you recall her name," Cormac said. Though neither of Diarmid's brothers lived with the same vivacity as he did, Cormac openly disapproved of it as often as possible.

"I remember the names of every woman who's company I've enjoyed," Diarmid defended.

Illadan scoffed from his watchpost outside their camp. "You do not."

Conan shot Illadan a warning look. "He does, and no one here wants to listen to him recite *that* many names."

Diarmid nodded appreciatively at his brother. Since they were young, he and Conan had always been close. They had fun with Cormac every now and again, and they'd defend him with their lives, but he had no notion of what life was really about. He was so caught up in the politics and wars and grand schemes of petty kings, that he forgot that life was lived by the moment.

"I wager that you can't go a fortnight without bedding a

woman," Dallan declared, earning a giggle of agreement from the lovely Niamh.

"I'm afraid you're going to have to be more specific." Diarmid wasn't certain whether such a wager would be worthwhile, particularly if he couldn't even touch a woman.

Finn responded without hesitation. "You can't do anything that could make you a father."

Tolerable. It would be far less fun, but at least he could still do something. "And the stakes?"

"Dallan and I will buy all your ale for the next moon, if you can manage it," Finn offered.

"And if I can't?" Diarmid honestly wasn't certain whether he'd make it or not, but for free ale, he'd give his best effort. Not to mention the joy of holding his victory over their heads forevermore.

"Then you buy ours," Dallan said simply.

Though Diarmid didn't relish the thought of losing that much coin, he knew it would be a powerful motivator. "I believe we have a wager." Perhaps he could find a lady tonight and...

"It starts tonight," Finn told him, interrupting his plotting.

Illadan, the leader of the Fianna, strode into camp, abandoning his watch. "It's time." He looked to Ardál and Dallan. "You cover us with your bows. Broccan claims there are fewer than twenty men at their encampment, and most will be sleeping. I will remind you that Brian has ordered Aodh be spared so that he has leverage for negotiations later on." Illadan's piercing hazel gaze landed on Diarmid. "You find the princess, since you're apparently so good with women. The rest of us will take care of Aodh's men."

The one downside—if he chose to see it as such—was that Diarmid *always* ended up minding the women. Normally, it would be a pleasure to spend time entertaining a lady. Even outside of his bed, Diarmid had always loved women. He found them to be clever and witty, without any of the posturing that so often accompanied his interactions with other men.

However, his last female ward had proved to be a tedious chore. Before following Aodh and the princess, the Fianna stayed in Thurles, believing that Aodh and his men had razed the village and overtaken the keep in an act of open hostility against Brian. During that time, Diarmid had, unsurprisingly, been charged with the 'management' of Brona, Queen of Thurles. 'Twas a long and convoluted tale, but in the end the Fianna learned that Aodh had been acting in self-defense. Thus, in spite of his capture of Princess Cara, Brian sought to spare the king and hopefully bargain with him in the future.

The men stood, securing their weapons. Diarmid's heart pounded, but his mind grew sharper, clearer. Though Diarmid made a point of enjoying his free time, these were the moments he truly lived for: the ones where his actions made a true difference in the lives of others.

He joined the Fianna to help Brian unify the disparate kingdoms of Éire, to defend the people from further incursion by the Fin Gall, the foreigners who continued to ravage their shores and lay claim to his people's lands. To fight for the folk who couldn't fight for themselves. Though he was born the son of one of Brian's rivals, Diarmid's commitment to Brian and the Fianna was absolute.

When they needed him, he would be there. Always.

Only moments after Illadan's call to arms, the Fianna disappeared from the small clearing of fallen logs, the graveyard of a massive oak. Roots and moss and lichen passed silently underfoot as the Fianna crept between the shadowed trees.

Darkness descended upon Aodh's camp.

And with it, the Fianna.

CHAPTER TWO

FOR THE TWENTY-THIRD night in a row, Cara couldn't sleep. Aye, even before she found herself the captive of a northern king, riding to what seemed the edge of the world. She knew her parents were up to something when they invited Aodh, her now-captor, to visit Thurles. From the moment he arrived in Thurles, sleepless nights had plagued her. Even with her suspicions, Cara hadn't come close to guessing their nefarious plot.

She sat up from her woolen blanket, spotting Aodh keeping watch near the remnants of their small fire. He was young for a king, especially a king of one of the largest kingdoms in Éire. Only a few years her elder, he had inherited the throne when he was nineteen—a year younger than Cara. She couldn't imagine the weight of that responsibility. Watching her parents manage one small village felt overwhelming at times. Aodh's kingdom held hundreds of them, and larger settlements, too. With his gentle manner and handsome face, Cara could have quite enjoyed his company in a different setting.

"Come," he called softly. "Sit with me."

When she complied, he offered her a small smile. This had been their ritual every night since they'd left Thurles. Some nights they chatted, others they sat in silence. Being a captive proved quite different than Cara had imagined.

"I suppose you're probably furious with me," Aodh said. "You've every right to be, but for what it's worth, I'm sorry for the pain I've caused you."

Cara studied him for a moment, watching the firelight breathe life into the strands of red that threaded his dark hair, considering his words.

"I'm not, actually." Her honest answer clearly surprised Aodh, who cocked an eyebrow. "Really," she insisted. "My family dishonored you, threatened your life while you were a guest in our home. They are the reason I am here now. They are the ones who deserve my wrath, and who deserved yours as well. I do not fault you for unleashing it."

"Even so," he replied gently, "I am sorry for it."

"I will admit that I'm not terribly thrilled at the prospect of marrying Eochaid." The elderly king of Ulaid was notoriously disagreeable. She'd heard countless tales of his harsh, sometimes ruthless behavior, and had little desire to be on the receiving end of it.

Aodh frowned at that. "I'll not lie to you, he's a bear. An old, bitter man taking out his regrets on everyone around him."

"He sounds lovely."

"But," he added cheerily, "he won't live long. And when he dies, you'll be a queen of one of the most powerful kingdoms. Though you'll lose the title, you won't lose the honor that accompanies it. You'll be able to marry whomever you wish."

"If he won't live long, then why marry me to him at all?" Cara asked, though she had accepted her fate the moment she'd agreed to come with him. Her mother's life had been spared because of her cooperation, though she was none too pleased with the woman at present.

"He'll live long enough to rebel and destroy my kingdom. I'm hoping he'll be placated by my offer of a bride, and subsequently too distracted to do any further damage."

Cara sighed. She had to admit that, as plans went, it was admirable. "You're a good man, to resort to marriage over battle in a struggle for power."

"Lives are too valuable to be thrown away on a whim," he agreed. "A good leader must know when the prize is worth the cost."

She opened her mouth to ask more about the remainder of their journey when Aodh went still as a stone, turning his head and listening intently. The air around them shifted, growing so heavy that she could almost feel it about her like a mantle. Aodh's green eyes roved the tree line before they turned to capture hers. And in those eyes, for the first time since they'd begun their journey, she saw fear.

"Run," he whispered. "Run and hide."

Gooseflesh spread down her spine, but Cara didn't move. "Aodh?"

"Quickly!" he shouted, rising and drawing his sword as men flew into their camp as swiftly as Achilles' Myrmidons descending upon Troy.

Cara bolted. She didn't even get a good look at the men who set upon them before she took off in the opposite direction, as fast as her legs could carry her. They'd encircled the camp, but she managed to slip past them as Aodh's men awoke and engaged them with impressive speed considering they had just been sleeping.

The forest fell away beneath her feet. Her legs moved faster than her feet could manage, and she tumbled over a branch. The sound of swords echoed from the encampment, sending her straight back to her feet. Only this time, she heard someone else's footfalls as well. She turned to see that one of the men had followed her. Even now, he closed the distance between them at an alarming speed.

Cara's heart hammered in her chest. She pushed her body to its limits, her legs burning with the exertion. Sweat beaded across her brow—the first time she could ever recall *that* happening since she was a young girl.

Still, the beast of a man caught her easily. His hand grabbed her upper arm, throwing her off-balance in her headlong sprint. She stumbled, lurching forward.

His arms caught her before her face hit the ground.

Then she smacked him. "Let me go!" she shouted, trying to scratch at him with her free hand.

He caught it, clicking his tongue at her. Mockingly. "That's not terribly polite, you know. Injuring your rescuer."

"Rescuer?" she repeated, inhaling with a gulp as she struggled to catch her breath. "What do you mean, rescuer?" He stood a full head taller than her, though she was by no means a woman of slight stature, and his broad shoulders and arms seemed to be built of solid muscle. Long hair fell in a disheveled mess to his shoulders, the top tied back away from his face. He kept a tightly shorn beard and mustache, and though he was handsome, Cara instantly recognized him as a rogue. He had an air of charm about him that always set her on her guard.

"Brian sent us to deliver you from Aodh," the man explained. "You are Princess Cara of Thurles, are you not?"

She stood tall, doing her damnedest to look down her nose at the giant, even though she had to lift her chin to do so. "I am. And you are?"

"Your rescuer," he replied with a devilish grin. "I already told you."

"You're a pain in the arse, is what you are."

The rogue actually laughed at her, as though common courtesy was nothing at all to him. "You've a sharp tongue."

Cara didn't have time for foolish games. "What's to become of Aodh?"

A smile played at one corner of his mouth. "Charming fellow, isn't he?"

"I asked you a question," she shot back, no longer able to hide her irritation and far too tired to care. "Is he to be spared?"

"Aye," he finally answered. "Brian has granted him clemency in light of your family's crimes."

"Good." Cara took a deep breath, praying for patience as she forged ahead. "And what of me? Will I return to Thurles?"

His deep brown eyes, the same hue as the blackthorn tree behind him, softened. "We're to escort you to Dyflin, that you might marry Sitric."

"Very well." Cara had long ago accepted that her marriage would be an act of strategy, not love, a fact that more than suited her. At least Dyflin was close enough that she could visit her sister from time to time in Thurles.

"That's it?" her irritating rescuer asked as they began walking back toward the camp. "You don't even look upset."

"Should I be?" she asked. "I've heard that Sitric is a kind and reasonable man, and I know this alliance is important for Brian. I don't see what there is to be upset over."

"It's been my experience that most women, even those who are prepared for marriage alliances, have some misgivings initially."

"Misgivings won't change my responsibilities or my future," Cara replied matter-of-factly. "I don't see the need to waste my time on them."

He regarded her with a curious look before extending an arm, as men often greeted one another. She took it, surprised at how warm his arm felt beneath her hand.

"Diarmid," he said, finally introducing himself. "Let's get you to Dyflin."

Cara fell into step beside Diarmid, thanking the stars above that it wasn't him she was going to be marrying.

CHAPTER THREE

"NIAMH!" RELIEF WASHED over Cara like the bath she so desperately desired. "It's so good to see a familiar face."

"Brian sent me along to act as your lady's maid," Niamh explained, walking over to where Cara and Diarmid had entered the encampment. "And in case of injuries. Are you well?" Niamh's eyes narrowed as she inspected Cara. Though she wasn't close to Niamh, Cara had been acquainted with her for the past six years.

"I'm just fine, thank you," Cara assured her. "Tired, but hale." Looking about her, she could just make out the faces of seven men, other than Diarmid, who stood about a reinvigorated fire. The band of warriors, apparently so talented they were sent without an army to retrieve her, were all giants. She realized, taking them in one after the other, that her original comparison of the men to Myrmidons was quite apt. "Who is the leader of this unit?"

A man to her right stepped forward. Tall and broad, as all of them were, he held an unmistakable air of command. "Illadan mac Mahon mac Kennedy, Princess Cara. I am leader of the Fianna."

Those names she recognized. "This is Brian's personal warrior band? And you are a prince of Munster, yes?" Illadan's father, Brian's brother, had been king before Brian, if she recalled her father's lessons correctly.

"Aye," he replied simply before gesturing to each of the men as he introduced them. “This is Finn Ulfsson of Ath Dara; Dallan mac Murrough, former prince of Laigin; Broccan mac Lorcan, commander of the king’s army and my cousin; and Ardál mac Shay.” Then he pointed to the last three men. “Diarmid, you’ve already met. These are his brothers, Cormac and Conan. All three are the sons of Cahill mac Conor mac Teague and princes of Connachta.”

“It’s a pleasure to meet you all,” she told them, shocked at how many princes stood before her. Brian’s cause had truly roused the kingdoms to action. Or perhaps he’d specifically requested royal blood. Either way, Cara was outranked by almost all of her companions. And she was a princess. “Thank you for delivering me from an unpleasant betrothal.”

“I’m afraid we’re simply swapping one betrothal for another,” Illadan replied gently. “We’re not to take you back to Thurles. You will marry Sitric, King of Dyflin, and we are to escort you there and see the betrothal formalized.”

“Yes, Diarmid mentioned that.” Cara felt the weariness deep in her bones. She knew she wouldn’t sleep well after such an eventful night, but she needed rest. “Will we be camping here for the remainder of the night?”

Illadan, as well as half the men before her, looked at her as though she’d grown a second head.

“What is it?” she asked, already guessing at the answer.

“It’s just that we expected you’d take the news a bit harder. Need more time to think it through.” Illadan repeated Diarmid’s prior comment.

Perhaps she needed to appear more put-upon, if only to get them to stop worrying over her. “I admit, I’m not terribly fond of the idea of marrying one of the foreigners who has killed so many of our own people,” she told them, trying to inject more feeling into her words and knowing that she failed miserably. It had been a long day, after all. “But I’m prepared to do what I must to help salvage the situation and prevent further bloodshed.”

“Sitric is a good man, though he can be a bit difficult at

times," Dallan, who stood with his arms about Niamh, offered.

"Aye," Diarmid agreed. "He's a handsome fellow who knows how to have a good time. You could do a lot worse."

Cara turned around to pin him with a sharp look. "Neither of those qualities implies that he would make a good husband. In fact," she mused, "I think they imply rather the opposite."

"You want to marry an ugly man?" Diarmid sounded truly confounded by the notion.

"I want to marry someone who will be wholly devoted to me," Cara admitted. "But, as I know such a man does not exist, I am content to marry whomever the king chooses."

Niamh looked up at Dallan, then turned to Cara. "Such men exist," she insisted. "Though sometimes they can take a while to find."

"I think you're better off marrying Sitric," Diarmid declared.

"And we'll all be better off if we get some rest before visiting him." In one swift statement, Illadan roused his men to action, setting up bedrolls and blankets.

After kissing Dallan, Niamh walked over and laid down beside Cara. Though they were of an age, Cara had always found Niamh's presence calming, as though healing ran through her even without the aid of poultices or tinctures. For the first time since Aodh had arrived in Thurles, Cara sank into a deep, dreamless sleep.

TWO DAYS LATER, they arrived at an inn on the outskirts of Dyflin, too far from the settlement to arrive before dark. The sun had all but sunk beneath the western horizon when they tied off their horses at posts in the stable yard. Cara walked into the single-story timber building, wondering how they could possibly secure enough rooms for all ten of them.

She hugged her satchel against her, squeezing the leather bag to ensure its contents remained safe. Aodh had allowed her a short time to gather any items she might wish to bring on her journey, and the first thing she'd grabbed was a book. Cara read everything she could get her hands upon, but her favorite stories were the tales of the wars in Greece and Troy. She hadn't been able to find her family's copy of *The History of the Trojan War*, a book she'd read a hundred times already, so she'd settled on the Aeneid. Aeneas' tale was grand indeed, but he was no Achilles.

The common room looked much like a king's hall, though only half the size of one and built in the style of the foreigners, or so she believed. She had never been in a Fin Gall home herself. Cara paused inside the doorway, her senses overwhelmed by the chaos of the room before her. A hearth burned bright in the center, much like her hall at Thurles, but no braziers lit the shadowed corners of the room. The heat of so many people crowded into one space, filling the tables and squeezing into every crevice between, hit her like a wave. The smell of lard, ale, and peat assaulted her nose.

"I've heard," a soft male voice whispered behind her, "that if you actually go into the room, the folk behind you can get out of the cold."

Cara didn't need to turn to know who'd spoken. Since that first night when they'd rescued her from Aodh, Diarmid had poked and prodded her relentlessly, apparently deriving great joy in her irritation. She didn't even turn to face him, tempering her rising ire so she didn't fan the flames. Instead, she searched the undulating crowd for the rest of her companions, finding them surrounding an agitated young woman. The top of her head only reached the center of Illadan's chest, but she stood there, hands on her hips, frowning up at him.

"I'm sorry," Cara heard the woman say tightly, her dark braids shaking along with her head, "but we have no beds left."

Illadan appeared to be arguing with her, though Cara couldn't fathom why. It wasn't as though she could will a spare bed into existence. Diarmid brushed past Cara, stepping firmly between Illadan and the woman.

"Allow me to apologize for my overbearing friend," he said, leaning toward her attentively. "I can see how busy you are, so we won't keep you. I'm Diarmid." He bowed to her with an absurd flourish.

The woman's shoulders loosened, but her lips remained tight. "Enat," she replied in kind.

"A pleasure." Diarmid winked at her—*winked*—and then the woman smiled. And Cara lost any respect she had for the beleaguered innkeeper. "Now, I believe I heard you telling the oaf behind me that there are no rooms left?"

"Aye, that's right." She crossed her arms even as her eyes softened, taking a good, long look at Diarmid.

"Have you tables open for a warm supper?"

"Aye," she answered. "But none as can fit all of you. You'll have to take two or three, and they're nearly full up already."

Diarmid nodded, leaning closer to the woman. "We'll be around for a while. If there's anything I can do for you, you know where to find me." The perusing look he gave the woman was so obviously suggestive that Cara could almost hear her own eyes roll in her head. "And if, perchance, any rooms open up, we'd be willing to pay you handsomely for them."

"You'll be the first person I come to," she promised. "Take any tables you can find, and I'll have your suppers sent out." Her blue eyes ran the length of his tall form before she smiled at him and returned to her other customers.

The other Fianna walked past Diarmid, either slapping him on the back or laughing as they ventured toward the tables. Cara just stared, her mind still processing the entire exchange. Diarmid's attentions had been so transparent, and so obviously for the purpose of securing them a room. And yet—

"You look surprised." Diarmid strode over to where Cara still stood near the doorway.

"I'm horrified that such drivel actually works," Cara retorted. "Surely no one would actually believe that you're being sincere."

He scoffed. "My dear lady, I *was* being sincere."

"You're telling me you would've offered your—your services all the same, regardless of the lack of rooms?"

"Of course," he grinned, his eyes sparkling. "I'm always happy to offer my services to any woman in need."

"How valiant of you," Cara quipped. "Happily, I shall never be counted amongst your conquests, nor forced to endure your misleading smiles." Prepared to have that be the last word, Cara took a step forward.

Diarmid blocked her, forcing her to retreat so she didn't run right into him. He moved even closer. Her back smacked against the hard daubed wall, her irritation bubbling beneath her carefully managed exterior. Even if she felt any sort of reaction, she'd be damned if she let it show. Diarmid put a hand on the wall beside her, using it to hold himself up as he leaned down.

"I believe you misunderstand me," he purred, his voice low. "First, in every scenario, *I* am the conquest. I never take a woman to my bed who isn't prepared to walk away the next morn."

He stood so close that for the first time since they'd met, Cara realized his eyes weren't just brown, at least not in this moment. They were honey-gold and amber, threaded with chestnut. They were beautiful. And they were focused entirely on her.

"Second, if you believe that I could really, truly, try to win your affections and you wouldn't be the least bit tempted, you're lying to yourself. And I'm willing to prove it."

Cara opened her mouth, because she absolutely had something to say about that, but he put a finger gently to her lips. "Before you go telling me how wrong I am, or to kiss my own arse, or whatever sharp-tongued reply you've invented, consider this. I have never—and I mean never—made that offer to a woman who hasn't accepted."

His thumb brushed over her bottom lip as his hand fell back to his side. And her treacherous body leaned toward him, as though aching for his hand to return. A warmth coursed through her that she'd not felt in a long time, not since she'd been in a very similar situation. With a very similar man.

"I apologize in advance for destroying your impressive record," she said, keeping her voice low to match his. "Now, if you'll excuse me, there's something over there that I *do* want: my supper."

She didn't wait for his response, ignoring his throaty chuckle at her tart reply. Ignoring the way it made her heart skip. Cara couldn't forget the last time she'd reacted to a man in such a way. A shudder rushed down her back as she recalled Torna. Just like Diarmid, he was all smiles, all kindness and warmth and charm. Until he got what he wanted. And then he was gone. She'd been a foolish girl then, believing herself in love before she even knew the meaning of the word. She wasn't a girl any longer.

And she'd not make that mistake twice.

CHAPTER FOUR

"YOU DID *NOT* proposition the princess! Diarmid, tell me you didn't."

The look on his brother's face was worth any trouble that would come of it. Cormac was livid. Diarmid sat opposite him, beside Illadan, in the only seat remaining between the two tables they'd overtaken. At Cormac's accusation, Illadan turned an icy glare on him.

"I was simply teaching her a lesson," he told them, knowing full well that neither believed him.

"You *cannot* bed her, all wagers aside," Illadan said. "We can't have her fawning over you instead of Sitric."

"I doubt that woman is capable of fawning over anyone."

"Turned you down, did she?" Cormac's eyes danced with amusement.

"I didn't proposition her," Diarmid shot back, taking a large bite of his stew before he said anything foolish. If only he could stop his thoughts as easily as their badgering. For, in truth, she was precisely the sort of woman he would normally pursue. When he stopped her in the woods two nights ago, he'd been struck speechless. Until she slapped him across the face, that was, believing him an attacker.

Of course, everyone in Thurles had told the Fianna of Princess Cara's unparalleled beauty. That was why she'd been taken, after all—she was a prize unto herself. Even so, Diarmid hadn't expected her features to be so striking, her scent so alluring. Her hair was the color of a raven's feathers, and her sharp tongue held all the bird's cunning.

Eyes the color of the sea, a vibrant blue-gray, glared at him with the same iciness that emanated from every inch of her. Aye, the woman was stiff and unyielding, though Diarmid would wager those pouty lips of hers would be soft as silk. Of all her many pleasing features, however, Diarmid's eyes were drawn most to her slim nose, with its rounded tip that was not quite upturned. Odd though it may seem, to describe anything on that frigid woman as adorable, that truly was the only word for it.

"Diarmid?"

He turned to find the innkeeper, Enat, smiling at him warmly. "Did you need something, dear?"

Though he had been rather forward with his charms in their prior conversation, Diarmid realized she was unlikely to suggest any tryst with him when he noticed a burly man glaring at him, taking silvers from someone for their supper. Her husband, no doubt. Diarmid enjoyed himself as much as the next man, but he wasn't about to bed another man's wife.

And he wasn't going to lose his wager on the first day.

"My husband found a room for your women," she nodded to the other table, where the ladies sat with Finn, Dallan, Conan, and Ardál. "I'm afraid that's the only one we can manage, though the rest of you fine men are welcome to sleep anywhere on the property. We keep the coals warm through the night."

"That's perfect," Diarmid replied with his signature grin. "Can we pay you double for your efforts?"

She smiled back at him. They always did—except Cara. "You can, but I'd prefer you lot kept guard. I've seen too many armies moving about, and you look like you know your way around a battle."

"We'll set a watch," Illadan assured her. "All will be safe."

After refilling their ale, Enat went to show Niamh and Cara to their room. Dallan followed, no doubt intending to sleep in front of the door. Diarmid would never cease teasing the poor bastard about going and falling in love.

"How do you do it?" Broccan asked from beside Illadan. Broccan was notoriously gruff, making him excellent at leading armies, but terrible at charming women.

"Well," Diarmid replied, forcing a serious tone, "it can be quite tricky, you see. In order for women to cooperate, you must be nice to them." He winked at Broccan, just to get a reaction from him.

Broccan gripped his mug as though he would throw his ale at Diarmid, until Illadan's hand stopped him.

"Must you?" Cormac glared at his younger brother.

Diarmid shrugged. "It's the truth. It's not my fault Broccan struggles with his temper. Illadan will support me in this—"

"I will do no such thing," Illadan grumbled.

"No?" Diarmid countered. "You, who is newly wed to a woman who wanted naught to do with you? You would disagree that kindness wins hearts? Or what of Finn, hm? He spent countless hours paying attention to a woman who'd fallen between the cracks, *showing her kindness*. Now look at them, married and all that nonsense."

The silence that followed his argument told Diarmid he'd claimed the victory, for the night at least. He stood, throwing back the rest of his ale and checking his sword before heading for the door. "I'll take first watch."

THE FOLLOWING MORN, Diarmid could hardly wait to get into Dyflin and stop this incessant traveling. Though he certainly made the most of his time on the road, he grew weary of riding from dawn to dusk, hardly fighting and not training at all. But as he sat eating porridge with the other Fianna, Diarmid realized it would be long past midday by the time they reached Dyflin.

"They're not ready to leave yet," Dallan reported again, returning from the room where the women had slept.

"What could they possibly be doing that would take this long?" Broccan grumbled.

"They wouldn't let me in to see," Dallan replied, taking a seat beside Diarmid. "But my sister always took hours to get her hair braided."

"How long do they require?" Illadan asked, eyeing the window to gauge the hour. "Sitric will want us before they dine."

"She said they were nearly finished, but I couldn't get anything more precise than that."

"It won't take that long to get into Dyflin," Diarmid pointed out. "Once we leave, that is."

"We cannot delay too long." Ardál stepped in from outdoors. "Rain is coming. Unless the princess has a woolen hood, all their hard work will be for naught when she gets soaked."

Diarmid stood, grabbing Dallan's arm as he strode past. "Come on, if we threaten rain they may hasten." Dallan muttered an oath in protest but stood to follow Diarmid all the same.

They hurried to the ladies' door, at the far end of a corridor that ran the length of the common room. Diarmid rapped his knuckle loudly several times. "Ladies, we come bearing news."

The door flew open, revealing an exasperated Niamh. "Well?"

"It will rain soon," Dallan told his betrothed as Diarmid craned his neck to peek around Niamh. "She'll be a drowned rat instead of a royal prize if we don't get out of here soon."

"What did you say?" Cara appeared beside Niamh, her dark brows furrowed against moon-pale skin.

"Did you apply powder?" Diarmid asked, reaching a finger to brush some of the white dust from her cheek.

She batted his hand away. "Of course, I did. Should I not dress my best before meeting the man I'm meant to impress into marriage?"

"Aye, but," Diarmid began, considering how to explain without it seeming an insult. He took in her carefully powdered and painted face, the pink dusting on her high cheeks, the red tint to her full lips. She looked bewitching as ever. No, her powders weren't the problem. It was her hair.

Those shimmering, blue-black locks were braided and pinned up, not a single strand left to hang about her face or shoulders.

"Well?" Cara pressed, folding her arms across her chest. Her full, rounded chest. Diarmid had to force his focus back to her face.

"I did my best," Niamh said softly. "I'm not trained as a lady's maid."

Diarmid dove in, against his better judgment. He was here to see her married to Sitric, after all. "It's just that I don't think Sitric is the sort who appreciates such a formal appearance. You'd be better off leaving your hair down."

Cara's blue eyes blazed, those tempting lips tightening into a thin line.

Beside him, Dallan choked on a laugh. "Are you actually giving a princess advice on how to present herself?"

"I spent several nights with Sitric when last he visited," Diarmid defended. "He and I have a good deal in common, and he always went after the women who appeared more…"

"More?" Cara demanded, her eyes looking about to burst into icy flame.

Dallan shook his head. "You've done it now."

"Fun-loving?" Diarmid tried. He'd wanted to say less uptight, but he doubted she'd take *that* well.

"Are you suggesting that a woman who wears her hair in braids cannot have fun?"

Diarmid ran a hand through his hair. "No, no," he lied. Not any woman, but this particular woman. "Of course not. You know what, forget I said anything. You look breathtaking either way."

The men excused themselves hastily, before Diarmid could dig a deeper hole. The women promised to be down momentarily.

"I've never seen you flounder in a conversation with a woman," Dallan commented quietly, before they rejoined the rest of the Fianna.

"I'm trying to help her," he grumbled. "Sitric won't be thrilled about marrying a woman made of ice, princess or not. You know that, too," Diarmid accused. "Why didn't you say anything?"

"Because, apparently, I'm wiser than you," Dallan retorted. "And because, no matter how loose that woman wears her hair, Sitric will see her serious demeanor the moment he speaks with her. It's not as though her hair could hide that."

Dallan was right, though Diarmid wasn't about to tell him that.

As promised, the women appeared in the common room shortly thereafter, looking radiant and ready for a royal visit.

"Diarmid!" Enat, the innkeeper, called, running to catch him before he walked out the door. "I wanted to thank you for all your help last night."

Diarmid caught Cara watching the exchange from the corner of his eye. And decided he couldn't resist teasing her further. "It was my pleasure," he purred, throwing Enat his most wicked grin.

"If you ever need to stay in Áth Cliath again, you come find me." Enat turned away, leaving Cara glaring daggers at him for the second time that morn. Diarmid determined that was simply her natural state—irritated indifference.

"Something wrong?" Diarmid waited for Cara to join him, walking into the street just behind him.

"Yes," she replied tightly. "You're despicable."

He pretended to drive a dagger into his heart. She didn't even smirk, only looked down her nose at him.

"Enat doesn't seem to think so," he observed when she didn't elaborate.

"Do you take anything seriously?" she asked at last. "How can you live your life so carelessly?"

Diarmid considered answering her honestly, telling her that he took everything—including his trysts—with the utmost seriousness. He had fun, but he took great care that no one's heart was broken in the process. He joked with the Fianna, but he would take an arrow for any one of them without hesitation. He made light of their quests, but he took an oath to King Brian, and he meant to keep it.

But telling Cara any of that would mean that her opinion of him mattered. And *that* was something he would never admit. Instead, he prodded her further.

"Some say the best cure for distress is humor," he quipped.

"Are you ready, Cara?" Illadan called, motioning for the princess to join him by her horse.

"Yes." She held her head higher than strictly necessary, picking up the hem of her gown as she walked away from Diarmid. "Unlike *some people*, I take my responsibilities seriously."

Diarmid shared an exasperated look with Dallan.

He'd never been more grateful to have escaped arranged marriages altogether. From the day he took his oath as one of the Fianna, Diarmid could only ever marry for love, meaning his parents could no longer arrange a match for him, or any of his brothers for that matter. And though he'd never much cared for the idea of having only one woman for the rest of his life, he was particularly grateful that he'd not been saddled with someone as cold and unfeeling as Cara.

Thank God for that. He watched Illadan help the princess seat herself on the horse, counting both his blessings and the hours until they were finally settled into Dyflin.

CHAPTER FIVE

THE EARTHEN EMBANKMENTS surrounding Dyflin rose up from what Cara could only describe as a swamp. The peat-filled bog cut swaths through the carefully-laid farmlands, until they came within sight of Dyflin. There, the earth itself seemed to fall away into the pools of dark, murky water that dotted the coastline, hidden between hills and trees.

Atop the embankments, a wooden palisade rose taller than any man she'd met—unsurprising fortifications for a people who had violently overtaken her own. Cara found it particularly telling that, in spite of the expansive trade industry in the harbor, the only side of the city without a gate was the one facing the sea. As though the Fin Gall knew their own kin may turn on them at any time, sailing across the frigid waters to lay claim to this godforsaken settlement.

"What do you think?" Niamh asked, riding beside Cara. "It seems..."

"'Desolate' is the word you're searching for," Dallan offered from in front of them.

Cara heartily agreed.

"It's not desolate," Diarmid argued from behind her. She wasn't the least surprised he chose to be disagreeable. "There's activity everywhere. It's bleak."

She and Niamh both turned around to look at him.

"Cloudy skies, the wailing of gulls, puddles of water blacker than a pond in hell. I'd go with bleak." He grinned at her, that same grin he'd used on the innkeeper.

And, as always, her insides melted. She decided sometime during dinner the night before that no matter how skilled he may be with sword or spear, that smile was his most potent weapon. Based on how often he wielded it, he knew that, too. Cara had absolutely no interest in Diarmid, beyond perhaps convincing him to consider reforming his ways, yet her body always reacted when he pinned her with that wicked, charming smile.

It irritated her almost as much as his juvenile behavior. Almost.

Split logs paved the roads of Dyflin, making a commendable attempt to keep the bog from overtaking the walkways. Most of the time, they succeeded. Occasionally, Cara's horse lost its footing on the slippery wood. All of the homes were built in the same foreign style as the inn, woven wattle fences separating the endless rows of adjoining properties. Everything, from the land to the buildings to the people, was so different from Thurles. For a town only a few days to the east and one kingdom over, it felt like a completely different island.

They wound their way gradually upward through the center of town. The tall masts of ships peeked above the sloped roofs of thatch and high palisade that hid the harbor from sight. The slow buzzing of saws and the clink of a smith's hammer sang a craftsman's song as they rode. The smell of brine, pitch, and pine filled every breath Cara took until they reached the far side of the settlement. Then it smelled of peat and roast boar.

A shorter palisade, of a height with many of her warrior companions, encircled a large group of buildings along the eastern edge of Dyflin. She counted at least two gigantic halls, easily twice as long and tall as the inn, and five other buildings as they entered Sitric's holding.

"Welcome, friends!" A tall, fair-haired beast of a man bellowed when they'd begun dismounting. "Dallan," their host made it to the grinning warrior in three long strides, embracing him like a brother. "'Tis good to see you again, cousin." Sitric's voice held a musical lilt that Cara found both unexpected and pleasing.

"'Tis good to be back again," Dallan replied, returning Sitric's embrace.

"And Finn!" Sitric turned cheerily toward the tallest man among the Fianna, whose sand-colored hair was nearly a match to Sitric's. Sitric spoke to Finn in a foreign tongue, leaving Cara to guess at what was said. When Dallan laughed at the exchange, she realized that he, too, must speak the language of the Fin Gall.

"You'll be wanting to learn it, I imagine," Diarmid whispered to her, walking to stand beside her as Sitric loudly greeted each and every one of them. Though Cara could have done without his ostentatious enthusiasm, she was impressed that he remembered each of their names, and a good deal more about each man.

"I suppose I will," she admitted.

"Most in his hall speak both languages," Diarmid added. "All the craftsmen and artisans come from the countryside and nearby villages, so the language of our people is just as common."

"How do you know that?"

The corner of Diarmid's lips curved upward. "Enat told me last night."

Before she could release the barb forming in her mind, Sitric reached her. Or, rather, reached *for* her. Instinctively, Cara took a step backward. Sitric's smile fled, his jovial attitude dissipating like a morning mist.

"You find me repulsive?"

Oh, Lord. She hadn't even said a word and she'd already botched her only duty. "No, no," she hurried. "You surprised me, I'm afraid. I find you quite charming."

He eyed her skeptically. In truth, Cara had no desire to embrace a man she'd only just met. She didn't even embrace her sister that often anymore. In an attempt to prove her point, Cara extended her arm to him, expecting him to bow or something equally respectable.

Instead, he pulled her into a vise-like embrace. Cara went

stiff, so uncomfortable she couldn't even muster the willpower to return the gesture. When he released her, she found nine pairs of eyes watching them apprehensively. Diarmid's pained look told her it was as bad as she'd feared. Niamh offered her a sad but encouraging smile.

Cara wanted nothing more than to melt into one of the muddy puddles littering this cursed town. Instead, she raised her chin and did her best impersonation of Diarmid's blasted grin. "You have a lovely home here," she lied, hoping it wasn't as obvious as it felt. "Perhaps you could show me around?"

"As my lady wishes," Sitric replied, some of the mirth returning to his tone. "Astrid!" he shouted into the nearest hall. He turned to Dallan. "That girl's never around when I need her."

"She's around," Dallan chimed in. "She's probably ignoring your bellyaching."

A stunning woman stepped out of the hall, certainly not the young girl Cara had pictured at Sitric's words. Though her features were quite striking, Cara couldn't take her eyes off the woman's fiery red hair, like embers glowing in a blacksmith's forge. "Or she's doing your chores," the woman, presumably Astrid, replied tartly. Her freckle-flecked face lit up when she spotted Dallan. She squealed as she ran to leap into his waiting arms. "Is Eva coming, too?"

"No," Dallan replied sadly. "Though she certainly wishes it."

Astrid rolled her lips into a pouty frown. "Perhaps I'll have to venture to Cenn Cora to see her. It's been too long."

"She would love that," Finn, Eva's husband, said, walking over to introduce himself to Astrid. "She can't stop talking about her wonderful cousin."

"You mean me, right?" Sitric interjected.

"No, I mean Astrid," Finn laughed.

"Well," Sitric pretended affront, "Astrid, as you're the favorite, why don't you show our guests to their quarters?"

"Happily." She flashed an exuberant smile at Sitric before ushering the Fianna toward one of the large halls.

"This way," Sitric held out his hand to Cara.

Cara looked at him, but didn't take it. She moved to walk beside him, keeping her hands clasped behind her back. If her dismissal offended him, this time he made no mention of it.

"Was your trip pleasant?" he asked as they turned to walk around the perimeter of his estate. In the distance, thunder cracked, an ominous grey cloud rolling in from the west. Sitric appeared unconcerned at the impending storm.

"Very, thank you." Cara took another look at the buildings before her, watching with some measure of amusement as Astrid appeared to give Cormac a talking-to. What he could have possibly done was beyond Cara. Of all the Fianna, he was the slowest to anger, the most patient. A gentle, quiet soul. Who had somehow incurred the wrath of the spirited Astrid.

"She's just making certain they know who's in charge," Sitric commented wryly. "I tease her constantly of behaving more like the hounds than a princess, asserting her authority with loud barking, but as you can see, it has done little to sway her. Perhaps she'll listen to you."

"If she's found some fault in Cormac, I daresay there's none who could sway her." Even from this distance, Cara could see Cormac's jaw clenching—something she'd never imagined possible.

Sitric tilted his head to regard her. "You find Cormac pleasing?"

"I find his temperament pleasing," she replied carefully. She'd already made such a mess of this introduction, the last thing she needed was Sitric believing she lusted after one of the other men. "He's reserved and soft-spoken, he makes rational judgments and seems altogether a fair man."

Sitric frowned. "I find him to be rather a bore."

"Why do you have two halls?" Cara asked, hastily changing the subject.

"One is for guests, the other for family. Both are a bit more extravagant than strictly necessary, but I had the land to add extra rooms."

"They're lovely," Cara told him honestly. "I can't wait to see the inside. I've never been in a Fin Gall home before, unless you count the inn to the north."

"Ostman," Sitric corrected gently. "We call ourselves Ostmen, not Fin Gall."

Cara mentally berated herself yet again, though she had no way of knowing such a thing without being told. "My apologies, I had no idea."

"I wouldn't have expected you to," Sitric replied. He didn't sound upset, but Cara knew this wasn't going well. "So how do you feel about the marriage?"

Cara forced herself to breathe evenly, not to show any outward signs of distress. She should have expected such a question, especially from such a seemingly open man. As far as she could tell, Sitric wore his feelings as he did his clothes—plainly for all to see.

"I look forward to it." She hoped he believed her. "Brian was smart to make such a match, and I think it will work in everyone's best interests."

Sitric's eyes narrowed. "Aye, it will," he agreed, though Cara sensed a riot of unspoken thoughts between them. "I admit, I'm not overly fond of the idea of marriage. For such a beautiful bride, however, I may be willing to make an exception."

Cara's stomach flipped at such an intimate statement. "You flatter me," she said, trying to brush away the uncomfortable topic.

"You are a virgin, are you not?"

"I beg your pardon?" Bile rose up from her belly. What did one say to such a brazen question? As her suitor, he of course had the right to such knowledge. But she had hoped this particular conversation would take place much later—certainly not the very day she arrived.

Sitric stopped walking as they completed their circuit, turning to face her curiously. "Well, now. That's interesting."

"What is?"

He leaned toward her, uncomfortably close. "Virgins blush when I ask that. You got angry." He gave her a knowing look, one that told her he as good as knew her secret, before opening the door into the hall. "Perhaps you have more potential than I thought."

Irritation flared in her veins as Cara floated gracefully into the warmth of the hall. Her mistakes may have made her more interesting to him, she fumed, but his superficial interest in her made him wholly unappealing. What had initially been an unpleasant duty was quickly becoming a thorn in her side. And that was if she could even get him to agree to the betrothal after their rocky introduction. Summoning what remained of her tattered dignity, Cara followed Sitric into his great hall.

CHAPTER SIX

MORE THAN ANYTHING she'd seen over the course of their journey, Sitric's hall took Cara's breath away. Warm, vibrant, and well-appointed, it was evident from the moment she entered that someone took great care with the maintenance of this grand building. Everywhere she looked, furniture and walls were covered with furs, silks, tapestries, and cushions. A large hearth fire burned bright in the center of the rectangular room, a boar roasting on a spit atop it tended by a pair of servants. On each end of the hall, a pair of large trestle tables ran length-wise down the central aisle. More intimate clusters of chairs and stools dotted with flickering braziers lined the edges of the room. Four doors stood equally spaced on each of the long walls, no doubt leading to private quarters for the family. The entire room glowed a deep, golden-flecked bronze, a wonderland of wood and firelight.

In the sitting area directly to their right, Dallan, Niamh, Astrid, and another woman held an animated conversation. The woman could only be Astrid's, and therefore Sitric's, mother. Her own blazing hair was a deeper, richer, more mature shade of the same hue as Astrid's. *Everyone* knew Gormla—she was the stuff of legends. Even in a small kingdom such as Thurles, where they hosted few guests and rarely had cause to visit Brian's court, even there Cara had heard tales of the queen.

"Mother," Sitric called, stepping over to interrupt a fit of giggles that was catching.

Gormla turned toward Sitric, smiling and rising from her fur-strewn chair when she spotted Cara.

"This is Princess Cara of Thurles," Sitric introduced. "Cara, this is my mother, Queen Gormla."

"Welcome to Dyflin, my dear," Gormla greeted her. "So, why is it that Brian chose you, of all the princesses in his domain, to wed my son?"

It seemed the trials of securing this betrothal had only just begun. "Because when the opportunity presented itself, he realized I was the best choice. And," Cara added honestly, "I believe he may actually enjoy arranging betrothals."

Gormla's mouth broke into a grudging smile, her eyes dancing. "You can stay," she whispered, turning back to her chair. "Sitric, I like her."

"You like anyone who jests over Brian," Sitric accused.

"Because it's a useful stick by which to measure how well I'll get on with someone," Gormla shot back. "Now, where was I?"

Cara still reeled from her brief but intense conversation with the formidable queen. Gormla had been born to the King of Laigin, Dallan's grandfather, by one of his Ostman slaves—a spoil of war. But according to the tales, the king fell in love with the woman, and promised to make her daughter a princess. The trouble was that no kings of Éire wanted to marry the daughter of a foreign slave, no matter who her father may be. So, he married her to Olaf, the self-styled King of Dyflin, forging an alliance with the invaders that lasted to this day.

When Olaf died, Sitric became king and Gormla married Brian—a marriage that ended only a few short years after it began.

"Your room is this way." Sitric's deep, rumbling voice pulled her from her trance. "Dallan and Niamh are two doors down," he added when they reached the door to the left at the far end of the hall. "I thought you'd appreciate more than just a wall for a barrier." His wink drove home precisely what he insinuated, and it was nothing Cara cared to think on any further.

"I realize it will take time to grow accustomed to one another," Sitric continued, leaning against the doorway into her room, "but I must ask, have I done something to offend you?"

"No," Cara replied. "Have I given you that impression?"

"You stay as far away from me as you can," he said. "You haven't offered up a single bit of information about yourself, though we've been speaking for quite some time now. And you only ask me questions about my holding. You say you are in favor of this betrothal, yet I have seen no evidence of it."

Fine. If he needed to be coddled, she would gladly oblige. Cara wasn't about to lose her family's home because of an uncomfortable conversation. "I dislike being too close to people—hugging, holding hands—until I get to know them well." She shifted her weight, suddenly uncertain what to do with her hands. "There, that's both part of the issue you're sensing and something personal."

"Alright, then," Sitric held out his hand, returning it to his side when he realized what he'd done. "Let's get to know one another."

He turned and walked out the door nearest her room, the one opposite the doors they had entered through. Cara followed, wondering precisely what he had in mind. She wasn't left long to her pondering. They hurried across the yard, past a small kitchen garden, to the second hall. Sitric threw open the doors with a mighty bellow, answered by the cheers and cries of the men within.

"Are the rooms to your liking?" he asked, sitting at the head of the table, grabbing a mug of ale, and gesturing for Cara to sit to his right. "I'm afraid Dallan is trapped with my mother at present. We shall have to drink without him." He offered a cup filled with wine to Cara.

"I'm afraid I don't drink," she told him sheepishly.

To his credit, Sitric made no remark, instead drinking the wine himself in several long gulps—to the infantile chants of the Fianna who sat about the table. Motioning a serving woman over, he ordered a cup of milk be brought for her.

"Thank you," she said, shifting her weight in her chair in a futile attempt to get comfortable.

Twenty-odd men and women filled the first two trestle tables in the hall, a perfect copy of the one they'd just left, a mixture of Fianna and Ostmen warriors in Sitric's employ. Three women that Cara could spy drank right alongside the men, wearing leather trews and linen shirts just like the rest of them. The lot of them laughed and drank. Several of the Ostmen boldly attempted a drunken ballad.

Cara stared out at the absolute chaos before her, wondering how she'd spend the rest of her days here. Perhaps it would have been better if her sister had come in her stead—Catrin loved such revelry.

"Now," Sitric turned to her, taking another drink of ale, "what is it you need to learn about me so that I no longer scare you?"

"You don't scare me," Cara corrected before she could think better of it. "I should like to know your plans for our marriage. Will you take mistresses? Will you include me in councils? Will you allow me to visit my family? What duties will be required of me, as it appears your mother and sister already run the household?"

Thinking of the marriage as her job, her responsibility, helped make the whole thing palatable. After her experience with Torna, she didn't relish the idea of sharing a man's bed again, though she knew it would be expected. Necessary, in fact, if they were to have children.

"*That* is what you must know of me?" Sitric's question brought conversation at their end of the table to a grinding halt. "What duties I intend for you within my household?"

With perhaps the world's worst timing in recorded history, Illadan sensed that Sitric and Cara were deep in conversation. And he apparently assumed it was a good thing, for he asked from the middle of the table, "So? Have you given any consideration to the betrothal?"

Sitric sat back in his chair and sighed heavily. "I have."

Cara's hands grew cold and clammy as she noted the look of regret that flashed across Sitric's grim features. Before the words left his mouth, she knew his answer.

"I'm afraid I must decline it."

"What?" Illadan's genuine surprise only made her feel worse. "Why?"

"I've decided that I've no wish to marry," Sitric declared, "especially because some king with an over-inflated ego decides I should."

"Perhaps it's best if we don't relay his exact phrasing," Diarmid suggested, breaking the silence that followed Sitric's statement.

Cara knew that was not the reason, though she was grateful for Sitric's discretion. *She* was the reason he decided he didn't want to marry. She saw his brows furrow deeper and deeper with each word she spoke to him, each time she pulled away from him. But she didn't know how to fix it, or, indeed, whether she even could. Unable to bear her embarrassment any longer, Cara excused herself and hurried to her own quarters.

Knowing she'd failed both her family and her king.

CHAPTER SEVEN

THE PRINCESS MAY have been made of ice, but Diarmid certainly wasn't. No matter how much she irritated him, Diarmid couldn't sit idly and watch her fail. The desolate look on her face when Sitric had refused the betrothal made his own chest ache. Not only that, but the tension amongst his fellow Fianna filled the room as each one realized how little control they had over the success of this mission. They had brought the princess to the king, aye. But not one of them could force him to agree to the betrothal. As he watched Cara flee the awkward situation, Diarmid decided he had to do something to help.

The question, was *what*?

"Sitric," Illadan began, his tone betraying his intentions.

Sitric held up a hand, interrupting Illadan. "I know what you would say, but I think it's best left for another time. You and your men, as well as the princess, are welcome to stay as long as you'd like. My home is your home until you are ready to return. But my mind is made up. The princess leaves with you when you go."

All the men had spent time with Sitric in one capacity or another when he'd come to visit Brian's fortress in Caiseal for Finn and Eva's wedding. They'd even fought by his side in the battle just before that. But Diarmid had always got on particularly well with Sitric. They shared a thirst for life that could not be quenched. They craved adventure, pleasure, fun. They lived through many of the worst things in life, yet they only saw the best. Perhaps his sense of kinship to the Ostman king was one-sided, but Diarmid guessed that it was Cara herself, and not simply the idea of marriage, that fueled his refusal. As Diarmid drank and laughed alongside the men, a plan began to form in his mind. One that would take both time and tact to implement.

First and foremost, he needed to get Sitric alone, to be certain his instincts on the matter were correct. He doubted Sitric would speak ill of the lady in front of a dozen men, but alone he may be able to pry the truth from him.

It wasn't long before the bell sounded for dinner, sometime in the midafternoon. They'd arrived at Dyflin midmorning, and in half a day the entire mission had gone sideways.

Diarmid's respect for Cara grew tenfold when, after that harsh rebuff not an hour earlier, she returned to join them for the meal. With her hair down. Not entirely unbraided, but she'd loosened some of the ties, letting a portion of silken black hair fall in waves down her back.

That something so subtle affected Diarmid's lust so profoundly was a testament to the fact that he should never have agreed to this infernal wager. If he'd been able to bed a woman in the past two days, the sight of some uptight princess letting her hair down would certainly not be getting his blood boiling. He threw back a long, deep drink of ale. And then another.

Cara, Niamh, Dallan, Astrid, and another woman sat at the far end of the table in what seats remained open, opposite Sitric and most of the Fianna. Diarmid spent much of the meal observing Cara and Sitric, their mannerisms, the looks they shared—which were few and frigid. He even watched how they spoke with those close to them. And in every conceivable way, they were hopelessly opposite. Where Sitric leaned to the man beside him, placing a hand on his shoulder and belly-laughing at a jest, Cara sat straight as a board, forcing Niamh to lean nearer to her for them to have a private conversation. Not once—not one time—did Cara's perfect lips break into a smile.

Distracted by his little game of observation, the meal flew past and what seemed like minutes later, folk began leaving the table. Some went into the seating areas that lined the sides of the long hall. Others got out game boards and went to find playing companions. Still others stayed put and raised their horns for more ale. Servants came to clear plates and cups and spoons, wiping the table with wet cloths and sweeping the wattle-covered floor below.

Diarmid strode over to Sitric, grabbing his arm and dragging him from conversation. "What say we forget this lot and go steal drinks from the alehouse and kisses from the maids?"

Sitric's roar of laughter had Diarmid grinning like a fool as they hurried from the hall. "Come," Sitric whispered, in the loudly hushed tones only a drunk man could manage, "I know a place you'll like."

They left the palisade that marked the borders of Sitric's holding, following a winding path of sodden split logs down the gently sloping hillside. The sun had not yet set as they wandered the streets of Sitric's town, folk still hurrying to finish their labors before darkness descended.

"This is the woodcarvers' hall," Sitric said, gesturing to a building as they passed. It looked much the same as Sitric's own hall—indeed, all the buildings did—except far smaller. "They train men from all over the island in intricate carvings."

"I've heard much of the skill of the craftsmen of Dyflin," Diarmid replied. And he had. Woodcarvers, leatherworkers, metalsmiths—all spoke of Dyflin as a mystical land filled with the most talented artisans. "More oft than not, when I compliment a smith on his work, he tells me he studied in Dyflin."

"Aye, he probably did," Sitric told him, pride filling his every word. "Hundreds come through each year. Some stay a sennight, others for months at a time. A few stay for good, though most prefer to bring their newfound skills back to their own kingdoms."

"Is it difficult? Managing the blending of two different peoples? You have many Ostmen in Dyflin, but I hear the language of Éire spoken just as much."

"At times." They arrived at a hall with its doors flung open, music and cheer emanating from within, a promise of merriment for the weary traveler. Or the weary king, in Sitric's case. Hung over the doors were two halves of a broken oar. "Brawls break out on occasion, but I work to ensure they've more cause to band together than squabble amongst themselves. Much of the time we have peace."

Everyone they passed greeted Sitric. Some bowed, others waved, a select few patted him on the back. Diarmid followed the Ostman to a bench in the back corner, in what would have been a seating area in Sitric's hall. Here, it was a smaller square table. They settled into their dimly lit corner of what was clearly a popular haunt.

"What about here?" Diarmid asked as a brown-haired woman, who looked just older than Niamh, appeared with two tankards. "Do you ever have drunken sailors or merchants causing trouble?"

"Never," the woman declared, setting the drinks down hard on the table, the frothy liquid sloshing over the side.

"That's right," Sitric agreed, winking at the woman. "Maeve here runs a tight ship."

"That's right," she agreed, glowing from Sitric's compliment. "We've never even had to hire a guard. The Broken Oar is a peaceable establishment."

Now that was interesting. "How did you come by the name?" Diarmid asked.

"My father told me I had as good a chance of running an alehouse as a woman as I had sailing a longship with broken oars," Maeve explained with a playful smirk.

"That," Diarmid declared, lifting the tankard in Maeve's direction, "is the best story I've heard all day. Here's to your hard-earned victory." Sitric joined him in toasting Maeve, who smiled and shook her head, promising more ale as she headed off to her next table.

"I know Finn's father is an Ostman," Sitric said, "but of all the

Fianna you are the most like any Ostman I know. Of course, there are some, like Finn, who are given to seriousness. But, the men who've come to Dyflin are all like us. We live our lives with bright colors, not searching for the subtle hues of the same shade."

"She is gray," Diarmid ventured. He knew he didn't need to speak her name.

"Like ashes from a fire that burned out long ago, yes." Sitric turned to him, more serious than Diarmid had ever seen him. "You understand why I cannot marry her. We have naught in common save a demand from the king to wed. We would both be miserable for the rest of our lives."

"Do you not add ashes to your swords to make them stronger?"

Sitric chuckled at that. "Only certain ones will work."

"I do understand," Diarmid admitted. "In all honesty, I don't know that I could marry her either. Have you tried telling her this?"

"Yes!" Sitric sat up, clearly enthusiastic over Diarmid's commiseration. "I asked her if I had offended her, why she was so cold and distant. Diarmid I cannot live with a woman like that. I spoke with her for but an hour and felt that she hated me. What would a lifetime be like?"

Diarmid felt equally relieved and concerned that he'd managed to guess at the true problem between Sitric and Cara. He was relieved because he now knew what needed to be fixed for the betrothal to progress.

Concerned, because there was only one person who could ensure it worked: him.

CHAPTER EIGHT

SEVERAL HOURS LATER, Diarmid and Sitric ambled back up the same hill to his hall. This time, however, the twinkling of stars above and the amber glow of hearths beyond guided them up what seemed a much steeper hill after a round of drinks. Sitric farewelled Diarmid, stumbling to the hall on the right, no doubt to fall into a deep, ale-fueled slumber.

Diarmid turned toward his own hall, where he planned to wait a short time before seeking out Cara. He needed to speak with her about what he'd learned, to propose his idea to her, but he couldn't have Sitric seeing him do it. Before he'd made it two steps, Cormac appeared, looking far less even-tempered than usual.

"Where have you been?" he growled. "We had an hours-long meeting and you were nowhere to be found. Do you take your duties so lightly?"

Normally, Diarmid would have made a comment aimed to further incense his overbearing brother. But a combination of ale and exhaustion made him simply speak the truth. "I took Sitric out drinking so that I could learn the cause of his displeasure. And because he's far better company than you."

"You've had too much ale," Cormac replied, bringing a hand to his chin thoughtfully.

"And you've not had enough."

Cormac hesitated. "Did you learn anything?"

"That you are a better match for the princess than Sitric."

"You must be drunk," Cormac scrunched his face at the very thought. "I wouldn't be caught dead married to that harpy, no matter how beautiful she may be."

Diarmid laughed. "I've never seen your temper pricked so quickly, dear brother. Perhaps Cara has gotten to you more than you think."

"Cara?" Cormac frowned. "I wasn't...never mind. So what did Sitric say?"

Diarmid glanced about to be certain they stood alone in the open yard. "He thinks she's cold and distant. Their personalities are too different."

Cormac sighed. "Some say that's a good thing, for balance."

"Sitric doesn't see it as a good thing," Diarmid told him. "He sees it as an insurmountable obstacle to happiness."

"We cannot change who she is," Cormac began, his voice defeated.

"But we can change how she behaves."

Cormac looked at him, eyes narrowed. "You have a plan?"

"I do," Diarmid replied, wondering just how much his brother would berate him over it. "I'm going to teach her how to behave around him, if she agrees. Get her to at least appear warmer." He waited for Cormac's sharp dismissal, for his logical explanation of why this was a terrible plan and how it would go horribly wrong.

But it never came.

"I can't believe I'm saying this," his brother began, "but that's not the worst plan. And it's far better than anything we conceived during our meeting."

It took several breaths for Diarmid to realize his brother actually *liked* his crazy plan. "I need to go speak with her soon, so she can remedy this before it goes too far awry." He turned to head into the family's hall, where Cara stayed, but Cormac caught his arm.

"Can I trust you with her?"

That he had to ask stung, but it was the nicest tone he'd ever used to suggest that Diarmid had no control of himself. And that wasn't even taking the wager into account. Hiding the pain of his brother's mistrust, Diarmid instead smiled at him. "I like her about as much as Sitric does."

"I'LL SEE WHAT I can find out from Dallan," Niamh promised as she slipped from Cara's room. They'd spent the hours following dinner dissecting every interaction Cara had with Sitric, and trying to decide what had gone wrong. She'd been polite. She'd been honest. She hadn't even jumped away when he'd pulled her into an embrace. She made every effort to be interested in his people, his kingdom. How could it have gone so wrong?

Cara began the laborious process of re-plaiting the few strands of hair she'd let loose for dinner. She always slept with her hair in braids, else she woke to a tangled mess that took hours to set to rights. It had been a pathetic attempt to make a better impression on Sitric. When she realized that her betrothal was failing, Diarmid's unsolicited advice rang through her head, and she'd decided there wasn't much left to lose. And Sitric hadn't so much as smiled at her when she'd made the subtle change.

Before working on her hair, she loosened the tight lacing of her woolen gown, slipping it off, folding it neatly, and placing it in the chest at the foot of her bed. With only her white shift on, she stretched, taking a deep breath and calming her mind after that awful day. She sat on the edge of her fur-covered bed, pulling her unbound hair over her shoulder with a resigned sigh.

Cara dropped the three strands of hair she held when a soft knock sounded on her door. Niamh must have news from Dallan, she decided, hurrying to answer it. She flung the door open.

To find Diarmid leaning against her doorframe, eyes wide as he took in her half-braided hair and gossamer-thin shift. Then that devil grinned at her.

"I take it you were expecting Sitric?"

Cara fought the urge to smack him again, as she had when he'd caught her in the forest. "I was expecting Niamh." She didn't dignify his insinuation with a response. "What are you doing here?"

"I need to speak with you. Privately."

"I'm not going to take you up on your presumptuous proposition," she declared, poking her head out of the door to see if anyone was still awake.

"They're all abed," he said quietly. "And I have a very different sort of proposition for you. I thought we could meet here." Diarmid gestured to the seating area right outside her room, a circle of four chairs around a small table. "Though, if you intend to wear that, we're better off in your room." His hooded eyes roved her body, pausing where the swell of her breast was visible beneath her shift.

Cara should move. Cover herself. Berate him for being such a beast. But the unexpected tightening of her belly distracted her.

Then she recalled the last time she'd experienced such a feeling, the memory finally propelling her into action. "Do you mind?" she hissed in exasperation.

"Not at all," he drawled, lazily lifting his eyes to her face. He was absolutely shameless.

"Are you incapable of thinking about anything other than naked women?"

"I've not bedded a woman in two days," he complained—as though this were actually some sort of trial. "I may as well be dead."

"Unbelievable," she muttered. "I'm going to have to, politely, decline your offer of a private meeting." She threw the door closed.

He caught it without flinching, pushing it back open. "The meeting wasn't the offer. I can help you win Sitric's betrothal."

Cara stilled. "How?"

"Do you want to meet, or would you prefer to lose your

kingdom and destroy what remains of your family's reputation?"

"You have one sentence to explain your plan," she agreed, narrowing her eyes at him. He was right, of course. She desperately needed to salvage her family's standing after her parents had broken countless laws in a misguided effort to curry Brian's favor. Brian had generously given her father's throne to Cara, as recompense for her sacrificing her own safety to save her mother and sister. But he'd made it clear that he intended to strengthen his alliance with Sitric by gifting Cara—and her kingdom along with her—to the Ostman. Her future, and her sister's, were dependent upon this betrothal.

"I will teach you to charm him so that he no longer thinks you a cold fish."

Cara choked back a laugh. "That's the most ridiculous thing I've ever heard. You truly believe that teaching me to toss him smiles and pat his back will change his feelings on something so important as a marriage alliance?"

"I do," Diarmid replied, not a hint of guile in his deep voice. "He believes you two are incompatible, that you don't know how to enjoy your life. Frankly, I agree with him, and since he and I are remarkably similar, I believe I'm the best one to help you change his mind."

"He said this to you?" Her head already ran with ideas of how to fix her blunder. "When?"

"When I took him out drinking after dinner. In fact," Diarmid added, "that would be a good way to start. Refusing his offer of drink was ill-advised."

Cara's heart sank. "If your advice to me is to take up drinking, then I'm afraid it's failed before it's even begun. There's no way I'll ever do that again."

"Do what?" Diarmid's eyes narrowed.

Cara worried her bottom lip. Too close. This was getting far too close to things she'd vowed never to speak of again. "I make poor choices when I drink," was all she offered.

"Yes," Diarmid agreed. "We all do. I believe that's his point.

But," he added hastily when she started to retreat into her room, "we can persuade him without you needing to do anything you're truly uncomfortable with."

He took one step toward her. The overwhelming urge to place a hand on his huge chest bubbled up from a long-dry well within her. A well she wanted to *leave* dry. It was safer that way. That such a short acquaintance with Diarmid already toyed with emotions and memories she'd fiercely guarded, that his closeness had aroused the thought of touching him, told Cara that no matter how reasonable his offer, her answer could only be one thing.

"Thank you," she whispered, "but I believe Niamh and I will be able to sort this out on our own."

"You won't have many more chances," he warned, his voice rough. "If you change your mind, you know where to find me."

"Good night, Diarmid."

He swallowed, his throat bobbing. "Good night, princess."

Cara shut the door before he'd even turned around, now absolutely certain that refusing him was the right decision. Not because she thought his offer unfounded. Not because his incessant flirting irritated her. Not even because she cringed at the notion of spending so much more time with him.

No, Cara knew she'd made the right decision the moment he called her 'princess'—and she realized she liked it.

CHAPTER NINE

THE FOLLOWING MORN, Niamh came to Cara's room at the first sign of light across the horizon to help her get ready for another attempt to win over Sitric. Of course, Cara didn't mention anything about Diarmid's late night visit. Niamh was helping her, but that felt too personal a discussion even for her newfound companion.

Cara retrieved her gown from the chest, changing into a fresh shift before Niamh set to lacing the deep blue woolen gown over it.

"Did Dallan have anything helpful to add?"

Niamh tugged on a lace. "He said Sitric is…" She paused, and Cara turned to see a thoroughly uncomfortable look on the healer's face. "He's very physical."

Cara let out a groan of frustration, about to bemoan the singlemindedness with which men apparently lived their lives, when Niamh continued hastily. "Not only with regard to true intimacy," she clarified. "Dallan said he loves hugs, handshakes, smiles. He likes there to be a warm, tangible presence in those he surrounds himself with. Dallan thought holding his hand and smiling might take you in a better direction."

"Oh." That wasn't so terrible as it sounded initially, and with time to prepare herself beforehand, Cara thought that might be something she could manage. "Thank you. And thank Dallan as well. I'll take that under advisement."

She'd had a few ideas of her own, as well. Once Diarmid had

hinted that she was too harsh, a 'cold fish' as he'd so thoughtfully put it, Cara wondered if behaving in a more feminine way might not help. The women she knew always spoke of gowns and embroidery, topics that to her seemed somewhat frivolous but made them happy all the same. Maybe Sitric expected her to be more like those women.

Deciding that her hair had no effect whatsoever on the outcome, Cara instructed Niamh to help her refresh the plaits and style them, much like they had yesterday. By midmorning, the two women were both dressed and ready for the day, slipping out of the room to find Sitric breaking his fast at one of the long trestle tables. Astrid and Dallan sat with him.

"Good morning," she greeted them, walking over to the table.

Dallan and Astrid mumbled a sleepy response, but Sitric just looked at her. Cara berated herself for already forgetting to smile. As an afterthought, she plastered a half-hearted grin onto her face.

What was wrong with her, that she couldn't even smile properly? That was a question for another day. Right now, she needed to focus on the task at hand.

"I had hoped I might persuade you to take me down to the harbor this morning," she said to Sitric. "I've never been to the seashore before, and I've heard the view is spectacular."

Sitric continued looking at her, his eyes narrowed as he no doubt weighed his response.

"You're not missing much," Astrid mumbled from beside her brother. "It stinks worse than a cess pit with all those ships and the sweaty men unloading them."

"I think it's a fine idea," Dallan replied, glaring at Astrid. "Go to the tower overlooking the harbor, and you'll have all of the magic with none of the smell."

"It still smells of fish," Astrid added before taking a heaping bite of porridge.

Sitric stood, his mind apparently made. "We will go," he declared, heading for the door. He didn't wait for Cara to follow.

They left Sitric's estate, back through the small palisade separating his home from the rest of Dyflin. Instead of following the log-covered road back down into the heart of town, however, Sitric turned to the right, following a road that skirted the outer embankment. Cara picked up her pace so that she walked beside him.

"Did you sleep well?" she asked.

"Very."

"Do you come look at the harbor often?" she tried again. That was a personal query, right?

He paused thoughtfully. "Not as often as I should. I venture down to inspect many of the shipments that come in, but I rarely wander this way for enjoyment."

Cara found that odd, considering how much he appeared to enjoy the rest of his activities.

"When I take time for myself, there are many other activities that come to mind first," he clarified when she didn't respond.

"Ah, yes. That makes more sense." Cara took a sidelong look at Sitric. He wasn't frowning or showing any signs of irritation as he took in the buildings and people they passed. This was her opportunity. "What sorts of activities do you enjoy in your leisure? I myself favor embroidery and sewing."

His brows furrowed.

Damnit. Cara hoped she didn't actually cringe when he looked at her. Before she could attempt any further conversation, they arrived at a set of steps leading up to a watchtower. Inhaling deeply, Cara could smell the brine in the air as they climbed to a viewing platform.

It felt as though the whole world opened up beneath her feet, falling away into endless blue. As far as she could see, bands of teal, turquoise, and every shade between reached toward the horizon, the sky barely distinguishable from the sea in the sparkling, crystalline abyss.

The sea carved a jagged line across the nearer shore, creating a sheltered harbor where ships and ferrying vessels drifted in and out. From her perch high above, Cara could see the shallow, sandy bottom beneath the waters. Instead of finding berth, several ships had simply run aground in the shallows.

"Astrid wasn't far off," Sitric said, his voice jarring her from her own thoughts. "Were we to venture much nearer, the smell of pine and tar would overwhelm any sense of the sea itself. The shipwrights make repairs from dawn to dusk."

A row of men moved like ants, hauling boxes and barrels off a ship with bright red sails.

"My father told me once that you get goods all the way from Rome here."

Sitric nodded, pointing to a ship with bright yellow sails. "They send beautiful, durable tiles that the monasteries and churches like, made of a reddish-brown stone. Porphyry, they call them. I find it to be a strange-sounding word," he chuckled. "Astrid favors the silks that come from farther east. We don't keep many, but you'll see a few about the halls. She's campaigning for me to buy her enough to make a dress of them."

"With her hair, it would have to be green or blue," Cara mused. "Perhaps a shade like topaz."

"I see you've already taken up her cause." Sitric turned to her, and Cara realized she should probably be smiling. By the time she'd managed it, he'd already turned away.

"Ready to head back?" he asked. The tightness had returned to his voice.

She needed to do something, and quickly.

Recalling the advice that she'd heard over and over, Cara thrust out her hand. He'd wanted to hold it yesterday, so hopefully one day later wasn't too late. "Yes," she answered, trying her best to really smile. "Thank you for bringing me here."

He took her hand, and before she knew what was happening, he'd brought his lips down to *kiss* it. Instinctively, she snatched her hand away.

Again.

Except this time, she knew a simple apology wouldn't fix the blunder. "I…I'm sorry." She stumbled over the words, too horrified at her reaction to speak. She hadn't even *wanted* to pull her hand away this time!

"I know that it's difficult," he began carefully, moving to lean against the side of the tower, staring out at the endless sea, "having to get to know someone quickly whom you've only just met. But I have a sense of people, you know?"

She nodded, not trusting herself to say anything yet.

"I don't think that we are a good fit, you and I. I know that you want this betrothal for your own reasons, and I would love to add Thurles to my holdings, but I don't think a life of this," he motioned between the two of them, "is worth it."

"I didn't travel all this way for you to give up before you've even given me a real chance," she told him firmly.

"If I'm to be tied to one woman for the rest of my days, she needs to be running into my bed, not away from it. Do you think, after any amount of time here, you could see yourself as that woman?"

No. Absolutely not. She'd never be *running* into any man's bed again. Trudging, maybe. Resigned. But certainly not with the enthusiasm Sitric obviously wanted.

"Give me a fortnight. Don't avoid me, let me keep trying. And I will prove to you that a marriage would work."

Sitric's mouth drew into a thin line as he grudgingly agreed. "A fortnight it is."

Cara hoped that would be enough.

CHAPTER TEN

DIARMID STRODE OUT to the largest clearing in Sitric's holding, sword in hand. After so long without a battle, his need to practice only grew greater. The other Fianna had actually gotten to swing their swords when they'd overtaken Aodh's camp. Diarmid had been sprinting through the forest after a cranky princess.

A cranky princess, who, if he was honest with himself, was truly the reason he felt like sparring at the moment. All he wanted was to get her married off to Sitric.

And out of his own head.

How he managed to be physically attracted to someone he found so irritating, Diarmid couldn't fathom. Yet somehow, he went from wanting to get as far from her as humanly possible one moment, to imagining how she'd look lying on his bed the next. Of course, seeing her in her barely-there shift hadn't helped at all. What really stuck with him, what truly gave him pause, was that when Cara noticed his gaze on her, pebbles had formed at the swell of her breasts. And when he'd called her 'princess,' those luscious lips of hers had parted, likely without her even realizing it. But Diarmid had noticed.

And Diarmid knew women. He knew that whatever cold exterior she presented to the world, Cara still had some fire buried inside her, probably much nearer the surface than any of them guessed.

The eight Fianna broke out into pairs to spar on the damp,

trodden meadow between one of the smaller buildings and the palisade. Normally, Diarmid sparred with Conan, who was the middle son, born between Diarmid and Cormac. They rotated often, of course, but Diarmid and Conan frequently paired off together without giving it much thought. This morn, Cormac walked right up to Diarmid, raising his sword. Diarmid grinned at him, partly in the hopes of unnerving his eldest brother, and gave his own sword a swing to test its weight.

"How did it go last night?" Cormac inquired under his breath as they circled one another.

"Terribly, as a matter of fact." In spite of his ill news, Diarmid kept his smile wide, his eyes narrowing in on his brother.

Cormac inclined his head, demanding further explanation. He let his sword arm relax.

"She didn't like my plan," Diarmid conceded. "And she wouldn't agree to it."

Before his brother could reply, Diarmid made his attack, earning a sharp oath from Cormac. He'd barely managed to block the strike. They sparred, each winning a bout before losing the next, until serving maids brought out baskets filled with food and a barrel of fresh drinking water. Covered in sweat and feeling more relaxed than he had in days, Diarmid joined the men as they descended upon the midday meal.

"I suppose this means we're not welcome in the hall until we bathe," Dallan said, sitting beside Diarmid in the grass.

"We're all moving too slowly, growing weak after so much travel," Illadan declared. "I think this afternoon we'll see what it's like to run a good distance through a bog."

Diarmid hoped their commander jested. "I think it will be a lot like sinking."

"Then I suppose we'll practice our swimming as well," Cormac replied from Diarmid's other side.

Damn. Illadan was their leader, but Cormac and Broccan were generally regarded as the secondary commanders. The three of them had been the ones to judge the initial trials, the grueling competition to earn a place among the Fianna. If two of the three said they were running in the bog, then it looked like they were headed to the bog.

Amidst the general grumbling of the rest of the men, Diarmid spotted Sitric returning from town. Their host didn't appear to notice them as he opened the double doors to his extravagant hall. Diarmid tore another mouthful of bread from the loaf he shared with Cormac and when he looked back up, Cara appeared. Also returning from town, her face unreadable as ever. She didn't head into the hall after Sitric, however.

No, she moved purposefully toward the clearing where the Fianna sat taking their repast, her eyes fixed on Diarmid. He decided it was safest to stay put and see what she wanted.

She stopped just short of the circle of men, who all looked at her expectantly. "Diarmid, could I speak with you, please?"

Diarmid looked toward Cormac, who nodded his head once. "Help the lady with whatever she needs, then meet us in the bog south of town."

Whatever she needed was going to take the entire afternoon, Diarmid decided as he rose to join her. He wasn't going anywhere near the bog, and he certainly wouldn't be running through it today.

He followed Cara to the guest hall, which was empty while all the guests sparred in the clearing and finished their meals. The hearth in the center had already been fed, the flames crackling happily as they devoured the fresh peat. Cara settled into a cushioned chair in one of the seating areas that lined the long, narrow sides of the hall.

Diarmid stood, not wanting to get dirt and sweat all over Sitric's fine chairs. "What can I do for you, princess?"

Her crystal blue eyes shot to him.

Oh, yes. It seemed she did like that name, he mused. He wondered if Sitric would ever figure that out, should matters improve. The thought left a bitter taste in his mouth.

"After giving it more consideration, I've decided that I do

wish to discuss your offer of aid, if it still stands." She sat straight as the back of her chair, her hands folded neatly in her lap, her face expressionless. Diarmid certainly had his work cut out for him. She was a perfect princess, but Sitric didn't want a princess. He wanted a bride.

"It does," he assured her, keeping his voice low. He doubted Sitric would be nearby, but he also doubted his friend would appreciate Diarmid's efforts to entrap him in a marriage he obviously didn't desire.

She bit her bottom lip, the first sign Diarmid had ever seen of true emotion in this woman. He couldn't take his eyes off the soft, pink flesh of her lips. Couldn't stop imagining how they might feel beneath his own.

"What did you have in mind?" Her hesitant question interrupted his wildly inappropriate musings.

"Before I know what we must work on, I need to know what happened with Sitric just now that changed your mind," Diarmid replied gently, knowing she'd not like that idea. "In fact, if you could relate to me what's happened each time you've spoken with him, that would help me greatly in deciding what to do next."

Cara looked down at her hands, rolling her damned lips together. "I can't seem to let him touch me," she whispered, her voice barely audible.

Diarmid fought the images that came into his mind at the word 'touch,' focusing instead on the intricate carvings on Cara's chair. "Touch you how?"

"At all." Her voice held a note of defeat he'd never heard before. "He tries to hold my hand, and even when I want to let him, I pull it away. Or, rather, it pulls itself away, regardless of my wishes. And this last time, when I finally offered my hand, truly determined to let him hold it..." She stopped, still staring at her hands, as though she couldn't bring herself to look at him.

Diarmid said nothing, simply waited. He knew she'd tell him when she was ready.

"He tried to kiss it, and it surprised me."

He found the thought of Sitric's lips on her hand oddly unsettling. "And you pulled it away?"

She sighed. "Is that even something you could help me with? I fear I've already made too great a mess of this to clean up."

"We have no choice but to try." Diarmid walked over to her, crouching before her chair so that their eyes were level with one another. "Your sister is counting on you," he reminded her gently. "And Brian ordered the Fianna to see you betrothed to Sitric, to help keep this tenuous peace in place. So, whether we fear failure or not, you and I are going to try to fix this." He stood, not wanting to create too serious a mood. "But first, I'm taking a bath."

A very, very cold bath.

CHAPTER ELEVEN

Cara ventured into the main hall for her midday meal while she waited for Diarmid to bathe. She let out a breath she hadn't realized she held when she poked her head into the building to find Sitric nowhere in sight. She wasn't frightened of him—not in the least. But she wanted her next interaction with him to go well, and for that to happen she needed to work with Diarmid first.

She was just finishing up when Diarmid wandered in to retrieve her, smelling faintly of sage, his wild, chestnut waves still damp. He wore a fresh shirt and trews, both of which fitted him tightly enough to display the mountains of muscle that lay beneath. They returned to the guest hall, where they were assured of privacy while the Fianna trained.

"Alright," Diarmid began cheerily, rubbing his hands together, "I propose we begin with hand-holding."

"I'm going to need you to clarify—" Cara thought for a moment, "Well, every part of that statement, actually."

"You told me that you wanted to let Sitric hold your hand, but that you kept pulling it away because it made you uncomfortable. Is that right?"

Cara nodded.

"I suggest that, as I practice with sword and spear, you practice whatever challenges you until it becomes second nature. So," Diarmid sat in one of the small seating areas, at a bench that could fit them both, and offered her his hand. "I'm going to be needing that hand of yours."

"This is ridiculous," she muttered. In spite of her protest, Cara sat beside him, placing her hand in his. Aside from the debacle with Sitric over the past two days, this was the first time she'd let anyone so close. Diarmid's hand, rough from hours of training, dwarfed her own. She felt the heat from his body, could sense the space he consumed beside her, could hear his steady breath.

"We could play a game," he suggested.

"Absolutely not."

"There's a child's game that involves moving your hands out of the way before—"

"Let's start with this for now," Cara insisted. Some long-lost part of her, the soul of the child she'd once been, screamed at her for being such a bore.

Diarmid nodded his head, but his feet began wiggling. Cara noted that he looked everywhere except at her.

"Are you incapable of sitting still?" she asked, sounding more irritated than she intended.

Diarmid turned to give her a brooding look. Except, Diarmid couldn't really look brooding, and Cara found it was more adorable than anything. "Alright, no games for now," he conceded. "But instead, we'll be talking."

Something in his tone told Cara that she wouldn't like the topic of discussion. "About?"

"Feelings." He grinned at her, that same, devious grin that normally caused a slight tightening in her belly. She didn't know whether it was the fact that she held his hand or sat so near to him, but this time a swarm of butterflies materialized somewhere in her middle. A feeling she'd not had since Torna. A feeling she'd not wanted again after. But here, next to Diarmid in the warm, quiet hall, Cara thought it wasn't as bad as she remembered.

"Have you always had trouble getting close to people?" he asked.

"Why should that matter?"

Diarmid squeezed her hand as he explained. "Look, you don't have to tell me all your darkest secrets, but I'm wholly invested in making this alliance work. And there is clearly something that made you averse to things like this." He gave her hand a jiggle for emphasis.

He was right, though she wasn't about to tell him that. Cara realized not long after Torna left that something inside her had broken, and she'd not had any interest in repairing it. She had far more important duties to tend to than forcing herself through her discomfort. "I haven't always had trouble with *this*," she replied, shaking his hand in return. "But I don't care to talk about it any more than that."

Diarmid's eyes narrowed. Cara could see that he desperately wanted to press her on the matter, that he deliberated doing just that. She was grateful when he changed the topic instead.

"My father is a stubborn ass," he said, his voice colder than she'd ever heard it. "He had no interest in us as children, and expected blind obedience the day we were old enough to carry a sword. That's why it was so easy for the three of us—Cormac, Conan, and I—to walk away. We respect Brian, and so we follow him."

Cara gave his strong hand a gentle squeeze. "My father was much the same," she admitted. "And my mother and I were never terribly close either."

"What of your sister?"

"Catrin and I were close when we were young." But once Cara withdrew into herself, they'd grown further and further apart. "I still love her dearly, of course."

"I know." Diarmid looked at her, his expression unreadable. "You'd not be here otherwise."

Cara wondered if perhaps she'd misjudged Diarmid. Not entirely, for there was no denying his roguish tendencies. But he did seem capable of taking *some* things seriously.

"What are you thinking?" he asked, his gold-flecked eyes staring straight through her.

"That perhaps you're not as irritating as I thought."

That grin again, as her insides fluttered and her heart picked up its pace. "I shall have to try harder, then." Keeping his eyes fixed on hers, he slowly lifted her hand.

She jerked hers but managed not to pull it away entirely. "What are you doing?"

"You said he attempted to kiss your hand, did you not?" He resumed lifting her hand, his eyes lit like the hearth glowing from the center of the room. When Diarmid's full attention fell on her, it felt as though the sun itself shone down, hot and bright and blinding. For an instant, Cara was put in mind of Torna. He wasn't anywhere near as charismatic as Diarmid, but his attention had made her glow all the same.

But as Diarmid's lips brushed the inside of her hand, any thoughts of Torna fell right out of her head. The man in front of her demanded all of her attention. His lips, firm and silky smooth, pressed a hot kiss in the center of her palm. A shiver coursed through her, one she knew he'd noticed.

"Do you know what I think, princess?" he purred.

Cara's core melted into a puddle of heat every time he called her that, a sensation she was *not* prepared to revisit.

"I think that behind that icy fortress you've built around yourself, is a fire that you can't quite contain. And it terrifies you." He spoke into her hand, his hot breath igniting the sensitive spot where his lips had been.

"And I think you're terribly full of yourself," she shot back, hating how defensive she sounded.

He kissed her hand again, her treacherous body preening at his attention even as her heart warned her to stay far away. "One does not preclude the other, princess." His hooded eyes issued a silent dare.

He knew what he was doing. *Of course,* he knew what he was doing. This man had bedded more women than Cara had owned dresses, she'd wager her life on it. He recognized the reactions he was getting from her.

"Why are you doing that?" she whispered.

"So you admit, it's doing something." He lowered her hand in his, resting them on the bench between them. "How do you feel about Sitric holding your hand now?"

She felt a lot better about Diarmid holding her hand, though she wasn't entirely certain that was a good thing. "Better," she decided quietly. "But that's not…I don't think that's how he was trying to kiss me."

"If it wasn't, then he's either a coward or a fool." The corners of his lips curved into a playful smile. "You should be more prepared, either way. Is there anything else that you felt uncomfortable with? We don't have much time before the bell for dinner, and you're going to need to make one hell of an impression."

Cara didn't much care for his reminder. "Conversation," she replied, determined to make the most of his help. "I never seem to say the right things. I've tried everything I can think of."

"Do you ever think things, then not say them?"

Cara rolled her eyes. "Of course, I do. If everything that went through my mind came out my mouth, then I'd sound ridiculous."

"You don't have to say *everything*, but try to say more things."

"That is not even a little bit helpful."

The door into the hall flew open as the Fianna returned from their training, smelling a good deal like the swamp they'd ridden through yesterday morn, and not looking much better. Hopefully they were on their way to bathe before dinner. Cara pulled her hand back into her own lap.

"Just tell him something about you, or answer a question that you'd normally ignore. Offer up some part of yourself so he can see you're trying."

Cara nodded, rising to go get ready for dinner. "Thank you."

The Fianna hurried back out to bathe, having grabbed clean garments from their rooms. Cara was grateful they'd been quick about it. Their stench alone would have sent their enemies running.

Diarmid grabbed her hand, grinning in approval when she didn't flinch. "Wear your hair down."

"I tried, it didn't work."

"You didn't let all of it down. No braids, or I can't promise we're going to get anywhere."

Cara glared at him. "Fine. No braids."

"I'll see you at dinner, princess."

CHAPTER TWELVE

DIARMID DIDN'T KNOW what to make of Cara. On his way into the main hall with the other Fianna, who no longer smelled like they'd brought the bog back with them, he decided that perhaps, as she'd so kindly put it, she wasn't so irritating as he'd thought. And, if she hadn't always had difficulty connecting with people, then it implied that something had happened—something she didn't wish to speak of—to change that. Diarmid felt his heart kick up several paces, his chest hardening in anger at the thought of someone hurting Cara so badly she'd stopped letting anyone in at all.

"Did it not go well?" Cormac asked as he slipped onto the bench beside Diarmid.

He couldn't remember the last time his older brother had sought him out as a dinner companion. They'd always had different circles of friends. Diarmid shook his head. "I think it went alright. I suppose we'll see soon enough."

Cormac regarded him thoughtfully, but said nothing. Much as Cara would do, Diarmid mused. As though summoning her with mere thought, the princess appeared at the far entrance. And Diarmid forgot how to breathe.

Those long, black locks were so dark that they somehow managed to glow a silvery blue in the firelight. Just as cool and defiant as the woman herself, they fell about her in soft curls and waves. The contrast between her black hair, her rose-red lips, and her sapphire eyes left Diarmid speechless. His gaze never left her as she took her seat near the end of the table where Sitric sat at the head.

A twinge of irritation burst within Diarmid as he watched Sitric smile and greet Cara. Though he had every intention of helping her charm the Ostman over the course of dinner, Diarmid found it difficult to continue watching the obvious lust in Sitric's eyes. So he turned back to Cormac, who was once more staring at him thoughtfully.

"You know," Diarmid offered up in a deceptively cheery voice, "it's irritating as hell when you do that."

Cormac smiled at him. "I know."

"So, are you going to tell me what you were thinking, or…" Diarmid stopped when he noticed a shadow pass over Cormac's face. Turning, he saw that Astrid and Gormla had taken their seats—Astrid between Cara and Niamh, and Gormla opposite them to Sitric's right. "I noticed you didn't get off to the best start with Astrid," Diarmid said under his breath so that only Cormac could hear.

"If Sitric turns on Brian—or rather *when* he does—that woman will be behind it, mark my words."

Diarmid sensed that this was a sensitive topic for his brother so, naturally, he pressed him on it, if only to take his mind off the breathtaking beauty who refused to leave it. "And this has nothing to do with the fact that she gave you a proper tongue-lashing the other night?"

"You're being ridiculous," Cormac snorted. "She's nothing but trouble, regardless of who she decides is the problem."

Though Diarmid knew his brother was the one being ridiculous, he was concerned that two people had accused him of such in one day. He dared a glance at Cara to check in on her progress. She listened as Sitric spoke with her, though Diarmid couldn't make out the topic of conversation through the din of the other guests. *Everyone* was talking. Loudly. What had begun as a gentle murmur of polite conversation, swelled to a roar as platters of food arrived and the meal began in earnest.

Cooked cod, soaked in golden butter and dressed in mustard greens. Hearty breads of every kind of flour Diarmid could name, steaming and warm. Roasted parsnip and onion, fried burdock, fresh pennycress. Strips of salted pork, wild mushrooms, and platter after platter of fruit and honey desserts.

After devouring half his meal in record time, Diarmid once more looked up to where Cara sat near Sitric. She'd lost his attention. Diarmid waited until she locked eyes with him, then motioned that she ought to speak with him. Her lips tightened and she inclined her head to Gormla, with whom he now spoke, facing away from Cara. She needed to interrupt politely. Warmly.

Diarmid decided Cormac would make a fine example. He made a show of placing his hand on his brother's arm until Cormac turned away from his conversation with Illadan.

"What?" he asked before following Diarmid's gaze to Cara. "Ah."

She frowned at Diarmid, but took an uncharacteristically deep breath. Then she placed a hand on Sitric's arm—winning his full attention and a brilliant smile in the blink of an eye.

That same, unfamiliar twinge shot through his chest again, making it ache with—Lord Almighty, was that *jealousy*? Diarmid immediately dismissed the idea. Why would he possibly be jealous of Sitric's smiling at Cara? He didn't even like her. Aye, she was stunning, but Diarmid had bedded many a beautiful woman. Admittedly, none so beautiful as Cara, but at least they knew how to relax and enjoy themselves.

Thankfully, even if he was tempted by her—which he wasn't—he had his wager to keep him from making any truly terrible decisions. And his unflinching dedication to his mission. And the fact that the woman literally turned her nose up at the hint of intimacy. And, most importantly, that she was an important pawn in Brian's political scheme to unite all the kingdoms. Thank God he had all those reasons to maintain the boundaries already in place, to keep his hands off Cara outside of helping her with Sitric.

"Your efforts appear to be paying off," Cormac remarked. The loud conversations about them ensured no one overheard. "Though you're looking at her the way Dallan looks at Niamh."

"I thought it more akin to the way you look at Astrid," Diarmid replied.

Cormac took that opportunity to glare pointedly at the redhead across from them, who stuck out her tongue in retaliation before turning back to Niamh. "If you mean looking at her as though I wish she were a man so I could challenge her stubborn arse to a duel, then perhaps."

"Niamh fought a duel. I don't see why Astrid couldn't. She certainly seems capable of handling herself."

"Indeed," Cormac grumbled, taking a generous bite of the savory fish.

"Friends," Sitric began, his voice rising above the myriad conversations across the table. "I've been thinking that perhaps we ought to make the most of your stay in Dyflin. I can think of no finer a visit than drinking, feasting, and fighting with friends."

The room went silent.

"Fighting?" Illadan repeated.

"Aye," Sitric's catlike smile reeked of subtlety. "I can't have Brian's best warriors growing stale in my keeping."

"We're flattered that you think you could dull our blades, Sitric," Dallan said to his cousin. "We've only been here two days, and we trained for one of them."

"True," Sitric mused, "but you haven't been in a battle—a real battle, not that skirmish where you rescued dearest Cara," he shot a pointed look at Conan, who had been about to protest, "in months."

"What is it you want, Sitric?" Cormac's even tone cut through the discussion.

"The same thing as Brian, in this instance." Sitric took a swig of his ale, looking from one man to the next. "When last I saw him, Brian mentioned that he was having some difficulties moving enough men north to properly convince Ulaid to bend the knee."

Everyone knew that, Diarmid nearly spoke aloud. Eochaid, the man to whom Aodh had planned to gift Cara, was perhaps even more a thorn in Brian's side than the High King himself—the one who held the title he so coveted.

"And this," Cormac continued, his voice giving away nothing, "has naught to do with the blood feud you now have with Eochaid, I suppose?"

"One does not negate the other," Astrid chimed in, her piercing golden eyes pinned on Cormac. "We can seek vengeance whilst furthering your king's campaign."

"The Fianna should not invade another kingdom without Brian's consent, regardless of his intentions." Cormac's tight tone brought a grin to Diarmid's face. That woman was easily getting the better of his brother—a feat he could watch all evening. He'd spent the better part of his childhood trying to upend his older brother's unwavering calm. And here Astrid sat, making it look easy.

"It wouldn't be the Fianna," Sitric said. "It would be the men of Dyflin. We could dress you as one of us, and none would be the wiser. We will arrive on ships, leaving no question as to who called the raid."

It was a risk, Diarmid knew, but a relatively small one. More than likely Sitric intended to raid some of the monasteries or small holdings along the coast or just inland. The likelihood they ran into anyone who would recognize them, particularly beneath an Ostman's guise, was low indeed.

"We shall consult amongst ourselves and give you our answer in the morn," Illadan declared.

Sitric nodded in agreement, but it was clear he'd hoped for enthusiastic agreement, not measured contemplation. He took another drink from his drinking horn, his mood subdued.

In the midst of the debate, Diarmid noticed Cara shifting her weight on her seat. Having Sitric frustrated by their conversation would not make her task any easier. He saw the same realization flit across her features, so he raised his hand just above the table, wiggling his fingers and giving her the most deliberate look, that he hoped implied she ought to grab Sitric's hand. The gesture would show her support, as well as some much-needed affection.

She shook her head ever so slightly, just enough for Diarmid to notice.

He crossed his arms over his chest and frowned at her, nodding once again toward Sitric.

Finally, she nodded. He saw her hand reach for Sitric's, which rested on the table beside his drinking horn. Sitric started, quickly realizing what was going on and flashing an encouraging smile at Cara. He whispered something to her and she nodded, though didn't smile.

When Sitric turned his attention to Illadan, clearly still urging him to join in the raid, Cara returned hers to Diarmid. He smiled at her, but he knew it wasn't his most convincing grin. He should be celebrating that they'd made progress after even one day, that perhaps this betrothal could work after all. Instead, that pervasive annoyance resurfaced, so much so that he could feel the blood pumping through his veins. Diarmid, inexplicably, couldn't stand to look at their joined hands on the table, turning instead to his brother again.

"Nicely done," Cormac said under his breath, keeping the conversation between them. "I think you should keep working with her. A few more days, and perhaps we can return to Brian with good news."

"I can do that," Diarmid agreed, finding he rather liked his brother's approval. He'd even enjoyed their intermittent conversations over dinner. "I can catch her tonight once everyone's asleep. It will be odd if I continue to miss training and she's always missing for part of the morning."

"I'll have Dallan and Finn on watch for you."

Instinctively, Diarmid turned back toward Cara to find that she was still staring at him, as though she hadn't moved. Had she been looking at him this entire time? Those icy blue eyes appeared ready to melt as she pinned him with a gaze he recognized. It was the same one she wore when he called her 'princess' or flashed her a mischievous grin, her lips parted just enough to drive him to distraction. Knowing no good would come of such thoughts, Diarmid made to stand. Cara's face fell.

So he stayed put and held her pleading gaze, wondering what on earth he'd gotten himself into.

CHAPTER THIRTEEN

HE WAS ALL she could look at, she realized in shock. Diarmid, not Sitric. When she'd felt her nerves take hold, all she had to do was look at Diarmid—to imagine touching his arm, holding his hand—and somehow everything seemed so much simpler. All her anxiety faded.

But her heart knew this was not necessarily for the better. Cara was thrilled that she had finally managed a positive interaction with Sitric. She was concerned that Diarmid already felt more familiar than anyone had in years.

Hours later, after everyone had left the hall save Sitric and his family, Cara sat in a fur-covered chair staring into the dancing hearth flames in the center of the hall, wishing she'd brought her book out with her, but not wanting to insult her companions by retrieving it. After so much noise and merriment, the silence felt deafening—so loud she could hear it as much as she'd heard laughter and discussion only a few hours earlier.

Niamh, Astrid, and Gormla sat around her, each reclining in one of the luxurious chairs. Sitric had spared no expense when furnishing his hall, and Cara could certainly get used to such comforts. His grand halls made her home in Thurles look like a hovel.

"I'm telling you," Gormla said insistently, though Cara had missed whatever began the conversation. "Brian won't come to Dyflin unless he's leading an army. He'll always summon us to him."

Astrid rolled her vivid golden eyes, a color that Cara had never before encountered. It was as though the Ostwoman were so full of fire that even her eyes exuded a heated golden glow. "Yet another way to show us who holds the power."

"Aye." Gormla's knowing smile held both patience and amusement. "But I believe it's more than a simple display of power. I think he's terrified to come here. It's been held by our family for so long, it's so entrenched in Ostman culture, that he knows it would be like coming to a different world. And you know how he feels about Ostmen."

Niamh leaned forward, elbows on her knees as her eyes narrowed on Gormla. "What happened?" she asked. "I've heard the songs, I've heard everyone else's stories. But, if you don't mind sharing, I'd love to hear it from you."

"Brian and I were too similar," she replied. "Believe me, I've given that marriage more thought than it likely deserved. Our personalities were too large to fit in one fortress. And I always felt that he was uncomfortable around me, as though he never quite trusted me."

"Oh, trust is the most important thing in a marriage," Niamh added a little too hastily.

"Before Brian, I'd have disagreed with you," Gormla chuckled. "I'd have said passion. Without a desire for the other, I wouldn't have believed it could work. But now, seeing how *that* played out, I believe you may be right, my dear."

"If you were too similar," Cara ventured, wondering why on earth she felt compelled to participate in such an intimate conversation, "then would you say people who are opposite one another work best?"

Gormla sat back in her chair, her eyes staring at some spot in the rafters as she weighed her response. "In some instances, yes. In others, no. The key is balance, so the opposite qualities must blend nicely, not push the other away."

Cara had just begun pondering whether she and Sitric were too different to ever blend into a happy marriage, when she realized with horror that Sitric hadn't been the man in her mind when she'd asked the question.

"Well, I'd best be off to bed," Gormla declared, rising and yawning. "It was a pleasure, ladies. I'll see you in the morn."

Astrid followed her mother, also yawning as they headed together to their rooms. Cara sat in silence, rationalizing her odd thought about Diarmid. It made perfect sense, really, that he would come to mind first. After sitting with him all morning, Cara felt more comfortable around him, which was what he'd intended. He was meant to help her grow accustomed to letting people in, so it was only natural that she thought of him when she thought of growing closer to someone.

And really, it had worked, hadn't it? Because of his efforts, his patience and persistence, Cara had begun the slow process of salvaging the situation with Sitric.

Niamh stayed put, waiting until Astrid and Gormla's doors clicked shut before scooting her chair nearer to Cara. "Sitric seems to be warming up to you," she whispered. "Do you think working with Diarmid helped?"

Cara's mouth fell open. Then she realized how Niamh knew. "Does everyone know?" Lord, how mortifying.

"No," the golden-haired healer assured her. "Only the Fianna. They all knew that Diarmid stayed behind to offer you some advice on winning over Sitric. Cormac was the one who approved it, after all."

"So I suppose they all know he's supposed to be meeting me again tonight as well?" Cara asked, ignoring the enormous blow to her pride. Every one of her travel companions knew she was so terrible at wooing a man that she required lessons in the most basic of interactions.

"You needn't be embarrassed," Niamh added, her brows furrowed. "Sitric didn't want a betrothal in the first place, to anyone. That's what Dallan and his sister both told me. Everyone knew he'd be difficult."

"That's very kind of you to say." Cara folded her hands in her lap, fighting the urge to twist her fingers together. "But that's not all of it, as I believe you know."

Niamh rolled her lips together, leaning even closer. "It would go a long way toward securing the betrothal to be able to hold Sitric's hand or hug him when he walks into a room—as that is just how he greets those closest to him. But don't force yourself into situations that make you truly uncomfortable. Don't change yourself until you lose sight of who you are."

"Thank you," Cara replied. That was just the trouble, though. If only someone had offered her that advice five years ago before she'd ever met Torna. Once he entered her life, he crashed through it like a storm, ravaging everything within her until he blew away entirely. By then, Cara could hardly remember who she'd been before, let alone remember how to *be* that person again.

When she'd sat with Diarmid, it felt as though a piece of that girl, the one she'd been before everything changed, fell back into place.

CHAPTER FOURTEEN

"WHO'S READY TO practice being incredibly uncomfortable?" Diarmid asked with a grin, rubbing his hands together as he strode into the hall.

Niamh giggled, shaking her head at his antics. "As much as it pains me to admit it," she said, turning to Cara, "there's none better to teach you to be charming than our Diarmid."

"Hey!" Dallan poked his head inside from the door behind Diarmid to glare at his betrothed.

Niamh shrugged, then hurried over to give poor Dallan a goodnight kiss. "I'll leave you to it," she whispered, disappearing into her room.

"Finn and I will be wandering about the grounds," Dallan told them. "Sitric took Illadan, Cormac, and Broccan down to the alehouse to try to win them over to his plan. If he comes back, we'll signal you." Without waiting for a response, he quietly shut the heavy oaken door.

Diarmid joined her in the seating area, this time sitting opposite her. He reclined in the chair, looking much like a wolf trying to pass as a dog. Even at rest, his powerful build and relentless charisma created a formidable presence. "So, how did it go?"

"You were there." Cara knew it was a sharp reply, especially for someone helping her, but she felt the need to put some distance between them.

For the briefest moment, she could have sworn his face fell. But then that grin returned, mischievous as ever. "I meant how did you feel about it? Did you feel that practicing it here with me prepared you well enough to endure it with our gracious host?"

Cara raised an eyebrow. "Endure?"

"It would be unfair to hold anyone to my standards of charm, obviously."

"Obviously."

"Good, then we agree. Now," he began, "we have two things that you should probably practice, and you're going to loathe both of them."

"Perfect," she replied tartly. "What do you propose?"

"Since we've made some real progress with physical contact, we need to work on conversation. Do you know much of teasing and bantering to endear your partner? Or of hinting at intimacy?"

"What do you think my mother taught me of courtship? How to seduce a man, or how to impress him with my knowledge of domestic affairs?" Cara couldn't believe she was even having this conversation. This wasn't the sort of thing anyone was normally *taught*. Normal people simply *knew* how to do all these things. Not as well as Diarmid, she grudgingly admitted, but well enough to get the job done.

"I understand your point, but, I know your mother, and it could honestly have been either."

Cara shot forward in her chair. "What?"

"I stayed at Thurles, remember?" he explained. "Dearest Illadan tasked me with keeping an eye on your mother so she couldn't get into any more trouble. And we didn't even *know* what she'd plotted with Aodh then. We just knew she was trouble."

"What did that entail?"

Diarmid shook his head at the memory. "Following her around everywhere. Listening to her complain about everything. Not to offend you, but it wasn't the most riveting assignment I've been given."

The conversation was already making Cara uncomfortable, she decided. "What's my other option?"

"Oh, we're doing both," Diarmid replied. "Probably at the same time. Then neither will seem so bad on its own."

Cara pinched the bridge of her nose. "I suppose I have no say in this?"

"If you're really, truly opposed to anything I suggest, we won't do it. But I wouldn't suggest it if I didn't believe it a worthwhile exercise."

She nodded her understanding. "And the other?"

"Hugs, of course. Have you ever seen that man enter a room?" Diarmid chuckled. "He even hugged Brian."

Cara did not like it one bit, even though she knew he was right. "Can't we work on smiling?"

"You should smile when you're happy. Not when someone tells you to. That will come in its own time."

"Fine," Cara grumbled, rising from her chair.

"Really?" Diarmid stood as well. "You're sure?"

"Everything you've suggested has worked," Cara told him. "So, I suppose I should start doing whatever you tell me to do."

A familiar warmth filled Diarmid's brown eyes. "If you say that to Sitric, I think that will get you pretty far into his good graces."

"I'm sure it would," she shot back. She knew he jested, but it wasn't a topic she found particularly amusing. "That's all men want anyway, isn't it? To bed women who tend to their every need."

Diarmid sobered immediately, putting his arms out. "It sounds like someone needs a hug."

"You're incorrigible," she mumbled, walking over to him and letting him embrace her. It felt much like hugging a pile of stones, his body hard, rippling muscle. His arms reached all the way around her, clasping behind her back and enveloping her in his warmth, in him. In truth, it wasn't terrible.

"I think you insult me every time you let me help you because it softens the blow to your pride," he whispered into her hair. "Ask me something personal, something that makes you uncomfortable to discuss."

Cara knew exactly what to ask. She'd wondered it many times in the days since they'd met, but she'd never had the nerve to say it aloud. "Why do you sleep with so many women?"

He took a deep breath, letting it out so close to her that she felt it like a summer breeze against her forehead. "Do you want the truth, or what I tell everyone else?"

"Both." That he had two answers told her she'd likely underestimated him yet again.

"I don't see the point in a life without fun, without making the most of each moment," he said quietly. "That's what I tell everyone, and it's true, but the reason I haven't ever once considered marriage is that I've seen too many bad ones. What if some poor woman ended up miserable with me?"

That didn't sound anything like Diarmid. Cara pulled back just enough to look up at him, noticing for the first time that his short, well-kept mustache didn't quite reach the stubble on his squared jaw. "Ironic, then, that you're pushing me toward just such a marriage."

"I suppose it is." One side of his lips tilted upward in a sad smile. "Your turn."

"My turn, what?"

"I get to ask you a question, so that you can practice sharing." He shifted his arms, so that they hugged her more tightly. "Did he hurt you?" His voice was low, tense. Dangerous. "Because I will actually go kill him."

She knew who he meant, though she'd not once mentioned Torna. And she believed him, though she had no idea what caused his sudden intensity. "He was a bit rough," she admitted, her voice shaking in spite of her efforts, "but he didn't hit me or anything like that."

Diarmid's body went rigid. "I'm going to be needing a name and a place, princess."

"I don't even know where he is," she whispered, the corners of her eyes tingling. Luckily, she'd shed all those tears long ago.

She buried her head in his chest as they stood there, embracing in the dim corner of the vast hall. Diarmid's hand stroked her hair, his heart beating so loudly she could hear it in his chest.

"I see why you might have a few things to say about my dalliances." He placed a finger beneath her chin, and to Cara's surprise she didn't mind at all. It didn't make her flinch. It didn't make her nervous.

It excited her.

He raised her face from his chest, staring at her so intensely she thought he might be reading her very thoughts. "I don't bed women by leading them to believe I want marriage. They know it is for one night because anything else would be criminal. What he did to you is unforgivable."

A tingle bubbled up her spine. She'd not even told him a thing and he'd been able to guess what had happened. What's more, he was the first person who hadn't tried to blame her for it. A weight she hadn't realized she carried lifted from her as, for the first time since Torna left her, she considered that perhaps she'd not done something wrong.

Cara, mesmerized by his words, by his scent, by his gaze, nearly forgot that he was an utter rogue. And that not two days prior he'd held another woman the same way he now held her. "But you bed married women?"

His hand fell from her face but his eyes never left hers. "I didn't bed the innkeeper," he told her with a smile. "We kept guard for her."

"But—" she'd berated him for doing so and he'd not corrected her. Indeed, he'd gone right along with her assumptions.

"It was more fun to prod your temper."

An odd whistle sounded from outside the front entrance to the hall. Diarmid's arms dropped from her waist, and he stepped away. Beside them, Dallan opened the back door. "Diarmid, out! Hurry!"

Cara didn't feel up to a conversation with Sitric, particularly if he were as deep in his cups as she suspected. She scurried to her room, happily the nearest one, and quickly shut the door behind her. Melancholy crept over her as she settled into bed, realizing that while she had enjoyed her meeting with Diarmid and would even look forward to hugging him again, the thought of being in Sitric's arms settled in the pit of her stomach like a meal gone sour. And though Sitric was kind and good-humored, he looked at her with either lust or disinterest, occasionally amusement or irritation.

Diarmid looked at her like she was his whole world. Every time.

CHAPTER FIFTEEN

AFTER HE'D CLEANED up from a vicious training session, Diarmid wandered to the main hall in search of Sitric. There was still an hour or more before the servants would start getting the hall ready for dinner, and Diarmid hoped to ask him if his thoughts on Cara had changed at all.

He hoped, quite selfishly, that they hadn't.

When he got to the hall, he was greeted by a wall of silence—a sure sign Sitric was nowhere to be found. He nearly walked straight back out, when he caught movement in the small seating area to his left.

Cara sat curled up on a bench, a blanket draped over her, a book open in her lap. She wore her hair down every day now that she'd started taking Diarmid's advice. It cascaded over her shoulders as she leaned over the book, as black as the sky at midnight, and with the same hint of blue. His fingers twitched at the memory of it beneath them. It had been but a brief moment when he'd hugged her, but it had been long enough to confirm that those gorgeous locks were just as soft as they looked.

"I wondered what was in that sack of yours," Diarmid said, sitting down in the chair across from Cara. "So, what magnificent tale did you haul across Éire?"

Her tempting lips thinned at his intrusion, but he wasn't about to pass up a rare opportunity alone with her. Or a rare opportunity to actually learn something about her. "The Aeneid."

"I've not read that since I was learning Latin," Diarmid

mused, "but I remember that I rather enjoyed it. Why did you choose to bring that one?"

Cara sighed. "You're not going to let me keep reading until you've gotten some answers from me, am I correct?"

"I'll leave you to your story soon enough," he promised. "It's not every day I catch you being interested in something."

"I chose this one because I couldn't find *The History of the Trojan War*. This was the next best choice."

"I'm surprised you don't like the Aeneid better," he thought aloud, straining to remember the characters and events that he'd read about when he was a lad. "There was rather a remarkable queen in it, wasn't there?"

Cara snorted. "Are you speaking of Dido?"

"That's the one!" Diarmid agreed with a grin. "She fled danger and founded her own city. That seems remarkable to me."

"She also killed herself when Aeneas left her," Cara reminded him, "in an absurdly dramatic manner."

"And that," Diarmid ventured, "doesn't—resonate—with you at all?"

Cara furrowed her brows, her adorable nose wrinkling at his suggestion. "Why should it?"

"I don't know the full story, but you sort of did the same thing when that bastard left you."

"That is not the same at all," she replied, vehemently. "He didn't live with me for years as my husband. He left me after one night. And I did *not* burn myself on a pyre of his belongings."

Diarmid managed not to overreact when she finally told him what had happened. Or more of it, anyway. "Dido stopped living her life after her heartbreak, in her way," he said softly, "and you stopped living yours in another."

Her glare broke as she digested his words. "You have no idea what happened."

"I don't," Diarmid agreed. "But I'd be happy to listen if you'd like to tell me." He had the ulterior motive of being unbearably curious, as well.

"You swear you won't go blathering it to everyone else?"

Diarmid scoffed. "I'm offended, princess, that you think I can't keep a secret."

"I liked a boy when I was young, fourteen, I think. Old enough to be thinking of marriage in the near future, young enough to find the entire process an adventure. When I asked him if he would court me, he said yes and almost instantly tried to get me into his bed. I refused, of course, since I hardly knew him. And he decided maybe he wasn't that interested in courting me after all.

"So the next year, my parents arrange a betrothal with Torna. He was handsome, charming, fun. Made my silly little heart flutter. And I didn't want to lose him like I had the last one. So when he inevitably mentioned that when you're betrothed, you share a bed, I agreed." She paused, clearly distraught with the memory.

"And you lost him anyway," Diarmid finished for her.

Cara's face fell. "I did."

"Because he's a bastard," Diarmid growled.

Before they could continue their conversation, Sitric returned to the hall, embracing Diarmid without hesitation. When their host turned toward Cara, Diarmid saw the resigned look on her face and knew she would at least make an attempt. She stood, setting down her book, and opened her arms in the saddest approximation of a hug he'd witnessed yet. They still had work to do there, he decided. Sitric hurried to accept her invitation, his surprised smile certainly a good sign.

Diarmid fought the instinct to rush over and separate them, ignoring the burning sensation in the pit of his stomach. He stood there the entire time Sitric asked Cara a similar series of questions over her book, pretending that it didn't bother him one bit. She wasn't his, he reminded himself, irritated that such a thought had even bubbled to the surface. She belonged to *Sitric*. And even if, God forbid, she'd somehow pricked his interest, Diarmid didn't do relationships.

As Diarmid wondered whether he had stood there brooding for too long, Sitric turned to him. "I was just coming to get my runes," he explained.

"Runes?" Cara asked.

Sitric grinned at her. "Wait here, I'll show you." He returned moments later with a small leather pouch held closed by a drawstring. "What do you wish to know?" he asked Cara.

The princess looked confused, clearly having no knowledge of the Ostman habit.

"Will we drink too much?" Diarmid asked, coming to her rescue.

"I don't need the runes to know that," Sitric laughed. "But I'll play your game." He opened the leather bag, gave it a shake, and dumped its contents onto one of the long tables.

Cara walked over to inspect them, her eyes narrowing as she studied the odd shapes and designs, each one on its own tiny wooden square. "Fascinating," she breathed.

"Well," Diarmid prompted, "what do they say?"

Sitric frowned, looking puzzled. "They say no. That can't be right."

"Maybe they're wrong," Cara suggested.

Sitric looked horrified. "They're *never* wrong."

"Will you explain them to me?" Cara asked, her eyes bright. "What do the symbols mean?"

Diarmid excused himself as Sitric and Cara bent over the table, unable to stomach the sight of them together. That was what he'd wanted, wasn't it? To help them build a stronger bond? To help Cara grow more comfortable around Sitric?

He never thought succeeding in his mission would cause him such discomfort.

It seemed Diarmid had his answer: Sitric's attitude toward Cara was improving.

And Diarmid didn't like it one bit.

CHAPTER SIXTEEN

"THAT WENT WELL, don't you think?" Cara asked Diarmid as he snuck into the hall to meet with her for another lesson. "Maybe we don't need to keep doing this. I think I've got the idea."

Aside from the sheer mortification of needing such lessons at all, Cara knew she was growing comfortable around Diarmid faster than she was around Sitric. A fact that may be counter-productive to their goals.

Diarmid crossed his arms, leveling her a disbelieving gaze. "Nice try, princess, but you're stuck with me until we have his name on a parchment beside yours. And," he took a step toward her, "while dinner went *better*, I think we've room for improvement."

"But he kissed my hand!" she argued. "And I didn't even pull it away this time." She'd been damned pleased with herself over that one. It had taken all the effort she could muster, but she'd done it.

"You looked like you wanted to cry."

"You said I didn't have to smile if I wasn't happy," she reminded him.

"And I stand by that," he agreed, his voice gentler. "But you need to at least look interested."

This was becoming more of a course in theatre than courtship. She wasn't interested in Sitric, not in the way Diarmid meant. And she didn't have to be in order to be a good wife.

"How do you propose to teach me such a thing?" she challenged.

That wicked grin, the weapon he used so readily, flashed at her. "Practice, of course. Go get your cloak, princess."

Pointedly ignoring the flutters that filled her stomach at the way that word rolled off his roguish tongue, Cara did as he asked, returning a moment later dressed for the outdoors.

"Will you at least tell me what torture you've planned?" she said, following him out into the chilly autumn evening.

"We've covered all of the pieces—holding hands, hugging, conversing. But when I watch you with him, though you're able to do all those things now, it still looks forced. So," he declared, offering her his hand, "we're going to put it all together. You've been going on walks with Sitric, yes? Where to?"

"I like to look out over the harbor," she replied.

Diarmid nodded, his eyes narrowing as though he were deep in thought. "Right. Here's what we're going to do—we're going to walk to the overlook, the same path you take with Sitric. I want you to pretend that you're walking with him, in spite of the fact that I'm far superior company. And I'm going to push your boundaries a little, do all the things we've practiced, but unexpectedly this time. Just as it would be with Sitric."

Cara groaned. "This is ridiculous," she muttered for the thousandth time since they'd begun this arrangement. "I shouldn't need to be doing this, practicing how to behave as a normal human being."

"You are a normal human being," Diarmid's gentle tone eased the tension she'd been holding. "And many people struggle with such things. There's no shame in practicing something to improve at it, no matter the skill."

Cara's stomach fluttered again, this time with greater insistence, as though attempting to pull her toward Diarmid and his kind words. In all her life, no one had spoken to her like that—like she wasn't broken or at fault. As though, even with all her sharp edges, she could still be embraced like everyone else.

They walked together in silence, taking in the settlement as it tucked in for the night. When the ascent to the overlook began in earnest, Cara realized that she'd been holding Diarmid's hand the entire walk. It had felt so natural, as easy as the journey itself or the amicable silence.

"Why do you enjoy the harbor?" he asked when they'd reached the overlook, a flat swath of grass with a view over the harbor and the obsidian sea beyond.

Diarmid laid his cloak on the damp ground and sat, patting the spot beside him.

Cara joined him, sitting far enough away that she didn't touch him.

"It reminds me of the Greeks sailing to Troy," she answered, watching as a ship with red sails tied off at a pier. "It's like seeing the story come to life. I can imagine them pulling up on the sandy beaches, ready for battle."

"Have you ever been on one?" His hand found hers, his rough palm enveloping hers in warmth.

"No." Cara couldn't take her eyes off their joined hands as he slowly raised them to his lips, pressing a soft kiss on the back of her hand. She shivered, but not from the cold.

"This would be a good time to ask me a question," he whispered against her hand, not taking his lips from it.

"What do you do?" her voice came out softer than she'd intended, matching his own intimate tone. "For fun, I mean. I read. What do you do?"

A disarming grin stretched across his face, his eyes dancing. "You know what I do, princess."

Cara nearly choked on her next breath. "That's your preferred pastime? Truly?" Aside from the discomfort of contemplating Diarmid in bed with another woman, Cara couldn't fathom anyone doing that for the fun of it.

"Is that so hard to believe? It's enjoyable for women, too, you know."

She very much doubted that. "Maybe for some women."

"For *all* women," he insisted, "so long as you're with a competent man, that is."

Until that moment, it hadn't truly sunk in that she'd be reliving that awful experience in Sitric's bed soon. Too soon. She wasn't ready for that again.

"Ask me whatever it is you're thinking," he demanded gently, turning her hand over and pressing a languid kiss against her palm. "Open up instead of keeping such musings to yourself."

"Do you think that Sitric is a man such as that?"

The playful fire left Diarmid's dark eyes. "I do."

Cara's belly dropped at the turn in conversation. "Tell me of the Fianna," she hurried, changing course from her unpleasant future. In spite of Diarmid's half-hearted assurance, Cara still couldn't see how what had happened with Torna could be so different as to make it enjoyable.

Diarmid didn't question her sudden change of topic. As the western wind picked up, rolling off the lively sea below, he told her of the trials he and the men had endured to earn their place among the Fianna. His face lit from within when he spoke of it, and with each addition to his tale it became clear that he derived great purpose from his position among the men. He took his oath seriously, and his bond with the warriors was stronger than she'd guessed. Once again, he surprised her.

His tale came to an end when the moon sat high in the night sky, pale moonlight leaping from wave to rippling wave in the chill winds.

"You're shivering." He reached both arms toward her. "And we haven't had our hug yet."

She didn't dread it, Cara realized in surprise. She didn't even hesitate, reaching toward him in return.

Diarmid shocked her by grabbing her waist and plopping her onto his lap. His arms wrapped around her, the heat from his body warming her back where they touched. Instead of fighting it, she relaxed against his hard chest.

"Would you ever court one of your women?" she asked. For

someone who claimed to only share his bed, he knew a great deal about courtship.

"I would not," he told her. "As I said, I have no interest in marriage, so courtship would be pointless. How are you feeling about sitting like this?"

"It's keeping me warm," she admitted, "and it isn't so bad."

"High praise indeed," he teased. "Should we try taking it a step further?"

Cara's stomach knotted at the thought, which meant it was likely a good idea. Clearly, she needed to work on whatever that might entail if she was nervous without even knowing the details. But she was curious over Diarmid's resolute resistance to relationships.

"I propose a trade," she said at last. "We can try a little more if you answer my question honestly."

A rough chuckle sounded from behind her. "What's your question, princess?"

"Why are you so opposed to a relationship? And don't feed me any of that drivel about other people's marriages failing," she warned. "Plenty of marriages do just fine. And a courtship is not necessarily a marriage. There must be another reason you won't even consider it."

A featherlight touch brushed the bare skin of her shoulder, followed by Diarmid's hot breath. His head rested just beside hers, his hands grabbing her hands and twining their fingers together. She felt his throat work as he swallowed, preparing to answer her question.

"I worry that I won't be able to keep the commitment, as I seem to make a habit of letting people down. I don't trust myself not to break her heart."

In spite of her better judgment, Cara gave in to the overwhelming desire to comfort him. He'd told her to say more of the things she thought, and this seemed as good an opportunity as any.

"You haven't let me down," she told him. "In fact, you continue to pleasantly surprise me." She turned, so that she could just make eye contact. "Perhaps you should consider our meetings practice as well, for when you decide to finally try courting."

He squeezed her against him, tightening the embrace. "Perhaps I should."

CHAPTER SEVENTEEN

THE FOLLOWING MORN, Diarmid joined the other Fianna to make another circuit around the outskirts of Dyflin. The town lay nestled between two rivers and the sea, with streams and rivulets reaching like spidery fingers through what little land connected it to the rest of Éire. The rich, earthy scent of peat permeated the heavy air, the fresh sea breeze the only respite as they ran.

Diarmid pushed himself harder than he had in weeks. He ran through the discomfort, his legs straining, his lungs burning. Every third or fourth step his foot sank into a puddle, sometimes up to his ankle, sometimes up to his knee. Mayhap if he ran far enough or hard enough, he could outrun his maddening lust. No matter how many times he told himself he could *not* bed Cara, certain parts of his body continued to disagree. Because, all bets aside, she was marrying Sitric.

"Bog running should've been one of the trials," Conan grumbled as he lost his footing beside Diarmid.

"It certainly tests my patience," Dallan panted.

"I'm going to find a bog near Cenn Cora so we can continue once we return," Illadan shouted from the front of the group, somehow not winded.

A murmur of opposition rose up, cut short when they ran through a swarm of midges and no one felt that protesting was worth inhaling one of the wee beasties. A light mist, teasing at rain, descended over the bay as the Fianna ran through the streets of Dyflin and up the hill to Sitric's holding.

Diarmid, along with the rest of the Fianna, headed to his room to get a change of clothes to carry to the river, crossing paths with the ladies just before reaching the guest hall. When his eyes caught Cara's, the same damned feeling rose inside him.

Apparently punishing his rebellious body hadn't fixed the problem. Perhaps he needed to slake his lust a different way.

He hurried down to the freshwater river south of the settlement with his friends, his brothers as he now thought of them, careful to avoid Cara. Though only he and Conan and Cormac shared parents, he had a bond forged in blood with the rest of the men all the same.

The frigid water, which should have chilled him to his bones so late into the autumn, felt clean as freshly fallen snow as it washed the muck and moss from his tired body.

"Alright," Illadan called, waving the men over to him near the center of the shallow river, "we need to have a decision for Sitric tonight."

"I say we go with him," Conan declared. "He's right. Brian wants to raid into the north, and would see it as a favor by Sitric."

"Brian hasn't approved our involvement there," Dallan cautioned. "If we're recognized and he's already managed to open negotiations, we could destroy any chance at a peaceful resolution."

"What if he retaliates and raids Dyflin?" Finn asked. "Would Sitric then expect Brian to send reinforcements?"

"That old bastard can't get his arse onto a horse anymore and everyone knows it," Diarmid said of the King of Ulaid.

"Even if he can," Cormac remarked evenly, "it would be Sitric's problem, as this is his undertaking. He's simply requesting our support."

"And, by extension, Brian's," Dallan added.

Broccan, Illadan, and Cormac exchanged glances. Coming to some sort of silent agreement, Broccan, leader of Brian's armies, stepped forward. "When Sitric visited last, Brian asked him to raid into the north by sea."

"Then why are we even discussing it?" Conan didn't try to hide his exasperation.

Cormac shot him a look of disapproval. "Because Brian ordered Sitric, not the Fianna. We didn't want to make such a decision without everyone's involvement, for if we decide wrong, then we risk Brian's censure. All of us."

"And what would you do?" Diarmid asked his eldest brother.

"I would join him," Cormac replied. "It would strengthen a tenuous alliance, perhaps even increasing our chances of getting him to agree to the marriage, and it would serve Brian's purposes as we understand them at present. Even if we discover later that he has, by some odd stroke of luck, changed his relationship with Ulaid, he would understand why we made that choice."

"And," Illadan added with a sly smile, "we didn't want to appear overeager. Sitric is our friend, and right now he is our ally, but we don't want him to mistake us as serving him in any capacity."

The men discussed the finer points of their decision to accompany Sitric on his raid, dressing and starting the walk back into town. Cormac grabbed Diarmid's arm, the pair of them falling to the back of the group until a good distance separated them from the other Fianna.

"How are things going with the princess?" Cormac asked.

"Fine." Diarmid looked to his brother, trying to gauge whether Cormac sensed his half-truth.

"You've been quieter than usual today," Cormac observed lightly.

"Everyone has quiet days," Diarmid hedged.

Cormac looked at him, his expression—as usual—gave nothing of his thoughts away. Diarmid always thought Cormac was wasted as a warrior. He could have been a druid, scholar, brehon, or king with his even temper and sharp mind. "Cara is as beautiful as the rumors say," he said, watching Diarmid carefully as he spoke. "I imagine that, once she warms to someone, she could be quite likeable."

"I'm not going to bed the princess," Diarmid growled at his brother.

"I didn't say you would." Cormac glanced at the Fianna, who were now nearly out of sight over the crest of a small hill. "I merely meant that any sane man could easily grow frustrated in such a situation."

"How is it," Diarmid grumbled, "that you always know what everyone else is thinking, without hardly even speaking with them?"

"I observe," Cormac replied. "You'd be amazed how much there is to be seen if you actually look for it."

"Well, wise, watchful brother, do you have any suggestion for what I ought to do?"

"Were I you, I would consider losing the wager and finding a willing serving maid."

Diarmid's mouth fell open. "*You*, who gives me nothing but criticism over my leisure activities, are suggesting I recklessly take a woman to bed?"

Cormac smiled at him. "I am suggesting that perhaps now is not the best time for the wager. Your situation is akin to a man who, drinking too often and too deeply, has agreed not to drink. Only for his friends to deliver him an entire barrel of the finest ale. Few men could resist such temptation."

Diarmid considered lying to his brother outright, telling him how wrong he was, that Diarmid had no desire for Cara whatsoever. But, for the first time he could recall, Cormac was offering him advice without judgment, genuinely trying to be helpful and understanding. They may not have had the best relationship in the past, but Diarmid saw an opportunity for the future.

"I don't know if I can keep doing this," Diarmid said at last.

Cormac put a hand on his shoulder as they walked. "We need you. Whatever you're doing is working. for a little while longer, and if you really need to, we can figure out another way after that. And in the meantime, find yourself a pretty maid. I will personally pay your debt to those two, as I feel partially responsible for you losing the wager."

Diarmid raised an eyebrow. "Partially?"

Cormac laughed. "And I'll take you out for a drink."

He could manage a few more meetings with Cara. It meant a great deal to his brother, who was counting on Diarmid, recruiting him for something meaningful for the first time in his life. He couldn't let Cormac down.

CHAPTER EIGHTEEN

"MORE ALE!" CORMAC called, waving over—yet again—the buxom serving girl. Serving *woman*, Cara corrected herself, for no girl she'd ever met had such sizeable curves.

"Unbelievable," she muttered, snapping a steamed mussel in half.

"It really is," Astrid agreed, not so quietly as Cara. "Two grown men falling over themselves because her breasts are the size of these rolls." She grabbed one of the honey oat loaves from her plate with much the same irritation Cara felt.

"They really are though," Cara looked between the loaves before them and the maid bending to fill Diarmid's drinking horn.

"Diarmid's had a long day," Niamh said, low enough that the men across the table wouldn't hear. "Let him have his fun. The maid seems to be enjoying the attention."

Aye, that she did. Her sugary smile and flushed cheeks filled Cara with the urge to snap apart all the shellfish within reach. The eager woman laughed as Diarmid whispered something in her ear, flashing her that grin that always set off a swarm of butterflies in Cara's stomach.

They were supposed to meet tonight, but it looked to Cara like Diarmid may be making other arrangements for his evening.

Diarmid never spoke to her at their meals, she realized as she continued to watch the garish show before her. In fact, since they arrived in Dyflin, he only *ever* interacted with her when he came to meet with her. He hadn't even looked at her or greeted her when she'd come into the hall to dine. Cara couldn't decide what irritated her more—that Diarmid apparently had no interest in socializing with her, or that she cared enough to notice.

The latter, she decided, breaking apart another mussel. She shouldn't care a whit whether Diarmid spoke with her, or noticed her, or smiled at her. She should be entirely focused on whether Sitric did those things.

"You should see your faces," Gormla called across the table, clearly amused by Cara's burgeoning anger. Sitric's mother turned to Diarmid and Cormac. "I don't think the ladies approve of your antics, boys."

For the first time the entire night, Diarmid looked straight at her. Cara felt his gaze course like a lightning strike through her. His hooded eyes, both cloudy and bright at once, searched her face before looking back to the maid. The look on his face roused a long-forgotten ache deep within her.

Cormac leaned over to whisper something to Diarmid, who frowned at him in response. Cormac shrugged, turning back to them. "I don't know why they should care at all." He speared Astrid with a dark glower.

"They shouldn't," Sitric agreed, placing his hand on Cara's and also giving Astrid a sharp look. "Let our guests enjoy themselves, sister. They've agreed to fight with us, after all."

The weight of Sitric's hand startled her, but she managed not to pull it away or jump. She didn't like the familiarity of the movement, the possessiveness of it. Cara kept her attention fixed on Diarmid, once again imagining it was his hand covering hers. Her racing pulse slowed, and she managed to relax into her chair a bit.

It grew more and more difficult to deny the very obvious and very problematic truth—that Cara didn't want to belong to Sitric.

And she didn't want that maid to belong to Diarmid.

She managed to get through the remainder of the meal, watching as Diarmid shamelessly pursued the serving maid, his brother doing his utmost to assist in the wretched endeavor. Cara waited until the plates were cleared from the table and the knucklebones brought in to rise from her seat.

"Stay," Sitric pleaded, giving her hand a gentle tug. "You should stay and play with us."

"I will another time," she promised. "I'm afraid I'm too weary tonight."

He smiled up at her, releasing her hand and turning his attention to his guests.

What was wrong with her? Cara brooded over her ridiculous feelings as she retreated to her room. Sitric was, by any standard, a remarkably handsome and charming man. He was young, fit, a strong warrior and a stronger king. He was one of the wealthiest kings, with access to trade routes the world over. She was nothing short of lucky that he had been the man chosen for her to wed. She should *want* to marry him. Perhaps that would come in time.

Or, perhaps those feelings she sought would hit her when the Fianna finally left.

When *one* of the Fianna finally left.

Trapped in her room, unwilling to face her riotous thoughts, Cara made her best attempt at going to sleep, ignoring the roars of laughter and the sounds of merriment coming from the other side of her door.

Some hours after she'd finally managed the feat, a soft knock woke her. Cara sat up, looking out her window and deciding it must be past midnight. Only one person would come calling so late, and she wasn't entirely certain she wanted to open the door for him.

After a second knock, more insistent sounding, Cara relented and went to the door, frowning at Diarmid. "What do you want?"

The hall behind him had gone eerily quiet, not a soul in sight. It seemed the games had finally ended. Diarmid didn't grin at her, and he didn't look the least shaken by her frigid tone.

"Sitric missed you this evening."

"I was tired," she lied. "Are you already finished with your most recent conquest?"

He stepped towards her, his wide shoulders filling the doorway. "You're jealous."

"What would give you such a notion?" She crossed her arms in an effort to disguise her discomfort.

"I saw the look on your face at dinner." His voice, normally honey-smooth, came out low and rough. "I know it well. It's the same one I wear when I watch Sitric put his hands on you."

Cara couldn't breathe. He stepped even closer, so near that she could feel the heat radiating from his body, could smell the intoxicating scent that made her want to lean into him.

"I'm here to marry Sitric," Cara whispered.

Diarmid's throat bobbed. "Aye, you are. That doesn't mean I have to be happy about it."

She forced herself to take a deep, shaky breath. "Why are you telling me this?" she asked.

"When I thought it was just me, that going so many days without a woman to warm my bed was creating this desire for you, it was challenging. But knowing that you desire me also, that's dangerous."

"I don't desire you," Cara retorted, too quickly to convince even herself.

"No?" He stepped fully into her room, shutting her door behind him. His powerful arms rose up on both sides of her, pinning her against it. "So you don't want me to kiss those pouty lips of yours, to taste you until you melt into my arms? To lay you down on that bed and let my fingers, my mouth, pleasure you until the only name you can remember is mine?"

He had won. Whatever game they were playing, Cara could hardly remain standing, let alone form a coherent thought after that vivid picture he'd painted in her mind. Forget the butterflies, her body was filled with fire, an aching inferno that wanted Diarmid to do every single one of those things.

"Ah," he purred, finally tossing her the wickedest grin she'd seen yet. "So you *can* blush, princess."

She saw now how he'd become the rogue of the group. "In my limited experience, none of those things are particularly pleasurable." Though he'd certainly made them sound that way, Cara knew better. She'd only shared her bed with Torna once, and that had been enough for her to learn that lovemaking was something to be endured at best.

"As I said before, whoever he is, he deserves a sound thrashing."

Cara couldn't agree more.

"So," he continued, "are you still going to deny that you were jealous? Or shall I keep going?"

"Fine!" Cara hissed. "Perhaps, I did not like watching you make eyes at that woman and smile at her. Happy?"

"Do you know why I went after her in the first place?"

"Because your lust is insatiable and your roguishness knows no bounds?"

"Because every morning when I wake, I wonder when I will get to see you that day. Because every time I do see you, it takes every measure of will that I possess to keep my hands off you. Because every night when I lay awake in bed, I imagine how you would look lying naked beside me. And I thought that maybe, just maybe, taking another woman to my bed would rid me of this infernal desire for you."

Cara's mouth had gone completely dry, her cheeks burning. "And did it?" She didn't want to hear about it, but she couldn't continue wondering.

"I wouldn't know," he answered. "When I should have invited her back to my room, I couldn't do it. All I could think of was that look on your face, and how I would feel knowing you'd bedded Sitric."

She couldn't take much more of this conversation. It was tearing her apart in ways she hadn't imagined were possible. "I don't want to bed Sitric," she admitted, hardly able to believe she was speaking such intimate thoughts aloud. "Every time he touches me, I endure it by imagining it's you."

His hand left the wall beside her, moving slowly toward her face. She didn't flinch as his rough fingers brushed her cheek, the muscles in his jaw going taut as a bowstring. Her eyes went to his lips, wondering for the first time how they would feel pressed against her own. When his hand cradled the side of her face, she leaned into his tender touch, his thumb caressing her. Cara told herself it was only because she'd been working with him, deliberately growing accustomed to his touch, that she now craved it.

But even as his gaze fell to her mouth, his eyes clouding with desire, Cara knew it was not so simple as that. In the same moment she thought he would finally kiss her, his hand slipped from her face and he took a step back.

"I cannot be the reason this alliance fails." His voice broke as he said the words. "I came here to tell you that I can't meet with you anymore, and I felt you deserved the truth of it."

She knew he was right. This was the responsible decision, creating distance so he didn't jeopardize all they worked towards.

Yet, for the first time since Torna, Cara found she didn't want to be responsible.

She wanted Diarmid.

CHAPTER NINETEEN

HE PROBABLY SHOULD not have done that. No, he absolutely should not have done that. The intoxicating combination of alcohol and desire got the better of him. He'd meant what he said, that he couldn't continue to meet with her, but he'd barely managed to get away without kissing her. Even now he could see the unmasked desire that had set her gaze afire. Aye, Diarmid needed to stay far away from Cara and the temptation that followed in her wake.

Conan's strike hit true, the flat of his sword smacking against Diarmid's arm. Around them, the rest of the Fianna sparred—a blessed reprieve from their runs through the bog.

"Where is your mind today, brother?" Conan taunted. "It's hardly a victory when you're not even fighting me."

"It's only a victory when I'm not fighting," Diarmid shot back, shaking out his sword arm. "Let's go again."

True to his threat, Diarmid bested Conan on the next two bouts, momentarily able to get his mind off the temptress. His victory proved short-lived, however, for before they'd even stopped for the midday meal she appeared outside the main hall, once again heading straight toward him.

"My apologies for the interruption," she called as she approached. "Might I borrow Diarmid?"

Had she not heard him last night? Had she not seen his struggle? Before he could refuse, Cormac readily agreed to her request. Diarmid hadn't spoken with him yet, so Cormac had no idea that he could no longer help the princess.

Unable to do aught else, Diarmid followed Cara to the edge of the field where the Fianna continued their sparring. The sound of steel striking steel ringing, ensured their conversation remained private.

"I need your help," she said, as though last night had never happened.

Diarmid crossed his arms over his chest. "Did you not hear me last night?"

She worried her bottom lip, the most vulnerable behavior he'd witnessed from her yet. "I heard you."

"Then you know my answer."

"Diarmid."

He liked the sound of his name on her lips far too much. "Cara."

"I can't do this without your help. Please." Her pleading look threatened his resolve. "At least walk with me and let me make my proposal. Like we did the other night."

"Fine," Diarmid allowed. He could manage a walk in the daylight. At a respectable distance. "But it will be a short walk."

"Of course," she agreed too readily.

The icy princess he'd traveled here with would have pushed harder. She was up to something. Ignoring his misgivings, Diarmid walked beside her toward the gate out of Sitric's holding. She turned toward the overlook, not speaking a word until they were nearly there.

"I walked up here with Sitric this morn," she said at last.

Dark clouds hung low, speeding toward them over the roiling sea. Diarmid felt it adequately reflected his current mood—brooding and ready to burst.

"Did it go well?" he asked. After his failed attempt at bedding the serving maid, Diarmid had finally understood the danger of their arrangement. He was developing feelings for Cara, only one step short of forming a relationship. And that was out of the question for more reasons than he cared to count.

"It did, I think," she replied. "But it got me thinking about my future with Sitric."

"I don't see what that has to do with me, princess."

"Well, you won't be here for it. Once the betrothal is in place, you'll leave with the Fianna. And I'll be left to deal with the truly uncomfortable parts on my own."

Diarmid's heart stilled. He ceased his study of the darkening sky to stare at her in genuine shock. "Are you propositioning me?"

A crimson flush swept up her cheeks, but she stood unflinching, the wind whipping her gown into a frenzied dance. "If I have this much trouble hugging and having open conversation, how much harder would it be to let him touch me? You're preparing me for everything except the true challenge—living with the betrothal. He said he wanted a bride who leapt into his bed," she choked out the words. "As it stands, I'd be running the other direction."

She took a step toward him.

The heavens chose that moment to open above them, a sharp, cold downpour soaking them to the bone. Cara's dress clung to her, her sodden black hair emphasizing the shape of her breasts with agonizing precision.

Diarmid's clothes were soaked, but his mouth had somehow gone dry. In a complete turnaround, she was actually propositioning *him*. Cara, the woman who couldn't bear to be touched and who'd done naught but chastise him for taking women to bed.

"You said yourself that you wanted to bed me," she pressed when he'd still made no effort to respond, "which leads me to believe it would be no great burden to you. And it would be a great help to me."

Aye, he'd said that—in the hopes of scaring her off from continuing their meetings. Not in an attempt to actually get her into his bed. He had, apparently foolishly, assumed that a woman who couldn't hold his hand without practice would be averse to the idea of anything so intimate. Lord, had that backfired.

He knew what he had to do.

But there was no reason he couldn't enjoy doing it.

Pulling her into his arms, he cupped her rain-covered cheek with his hand. He savored the feel of her soft, feminine body pressed against him.

"I do want to bed you," he agreed. "I meant what I said. And if I took you, we would spend hour after hour reversing whatever misconceptions you have about your ability to experience pleasure." He ran his thumb over her parted lips, his heart hammering louder than the torrential rains. "You would fall apart in my arms over and over until I'd ruined you for any other man. Oh, yes, princess, I do want to bed you," he repeated, letting his hand drop to his side, "which is exactly why I cannot."

Using all his remaining willpower, Diarmid escorted Cara back to the holding, wondering whether he'd be able to endure another such request.

And praying he need never find out.

CHAPTER TWENTY

"I FEEL THAT we've been making real progress," Sitric declared, taking Cara's hand in his as they returned from the harbor. After Cara had asked Gormla and Astrid a thousand questions regarding the ships, the water, the materials that came and went, and anything else she could imagine relating to Dyflin's legendary trade industry, the women had told Sitric that he needed to take her down to the docks for a proper tour of them.

It had been three days since Diarmid came to her room. Two days since she'd learned that the reason he avoided her was not that he had no interest in her—it was just the opposite. And now, every time they crossed paths and he turned away, every time he didn't smile at her, she remembered how it felt to be pressed against him and his arms. She remembered those forbidden, seductive words he'd uttered, and she wished for the first time in her life that she'd not been born a princess.

That she could marry whomever she chose.

"Enough progress for a betrothal?" she ventured, though her heart wasn't in the query.

"We have ten days left," Sitric replied. Though his voice was pleasing, it didn't heat her blood like Diarmid's did, she noted.

Cara didn't like that even after she let Sitric nearer, he still felt the need to wait the full fortnight to reach a decision.

They turned down a bend in the plank-covered road, the brightly colored sails and swooping gulls disappearing as they climbed toward Sitric's holding.

"Is there aught I can do to persuade you further?" She thought this outing had gone better. He'd held her hand—though she was grateful he hadn't attempted to kiss it again. She'd managed a conversation without causing him obvious irritation. He'd even smiled at her once or twice.

"There is," he told her hesitantly.

She looked at him, raising a brow. He'd better not ask her to bed him. It hadn't worked the last time, when Torna had insisted that's what happened when you were betrothed, and she wasn't about to fall for that nonsense again.

"If you can bring yourself to kiss me, that would convince me that this marriage stands a chance at being more than a sentence to misery for us both."

Well, it was better than bedding him. "If you don't mind my asking, why would that convince you?"

His mouth lifted into a half-smile. "You can tell a lot about a person, and how you feel about them, from a kiss."

A knot formed in Cara's middle, rising to her chest along with a growing sense of panic. If the kiss went terribly, that would be it. All her efforts would be for naught, all hope of the betrothal lost.

Their final turn approached, the one that led up the hill to the two great halls inside the circling palisade. Cara knew she'd not be able to finish this herself.

"I'm going to have a walk around the settlement, if you don't mind."

Sitric halted. "Do you wish company or solace?"

His kindness made her wish he was the one she wanted. "Solace, if that's alright. Thank you for taking me to the harbor today," she added, hoping he heard the real gratitude in her voice. "I truly enjoyed it."

"We can return any time you wish," he told her, faring her well before leaving her to continue on.

Cara knew she couldn't muster up the courage to kiss Sitric without help.

And she knew help was just outside of town, washing in the river after a run through the bog.

DIARMID ARRIVED AT the conclusion, after two days of avoiding Cara, in spite of her hunting him down yesterday afternoon, that he desperately needed to lose the wager, for his own sanity. No amount of sparring, no amount of running through the bogs, or taking cold baths in the river, or any number of other things he'd attempted had managed to keep his mind off the princess.

He'd gone to her room, believing that when he admitted his desire for her she would do what she did best—build a wall to keep him out. He'd been counting on it, in fact. Having Cara deny him outright would've gone a long way to assuaging his obsession with her.

But the damned woman hadn't done anything of the kind—just the opposite, in fact. He'd touched her without warning, his final attempt to get her to push back. Instead, she'd leaned into him. She'd looked at him like she wanted him to do every single wicked thing he'd suggested and then some.

And he nearly had. The moment he realized she wanted him to kiss her was the moment he knew he had to leave before he ruined everything.

Including Cara.

He hadn't told Cormac the details of that night, or that he'd halted their meetings. He made excuses each night, but he couldn't bring himself to tell his brother he'd failed. He'd let him down the one time Cormac had come to him for help. Everyone depended on him, and Diarmid, lover of women, couldn't stand to spend time with one.

They were just finishing a wash after another run through the bog—an exercise their fearless leader had become entirely too fond of, to Diarmid's way of thinking—when Cara appeared along the riverbank. Diarmid had already put on his trews, thankfully, but hadn't even picked up his shirt.

It wasn't uncommon for men and women to wash together in the rivers and streams, but the nobility did it with far less frequency than the peasants. Families who could afford bathing tubs had little need for public washing, unless of course they'd gone running through a bog and were so covered in muck they would've felt badly for the tub.

For a moment, Diarmid wondered if she'd ever even seen a man undressed. Then he remembered Torna, and rage filled him faster than a lake filled a broken dam. As much as he desired Cara, and knew that meant he should stay as far away as he could get, he also wanted time with her to correct whatever horrid idea that bastard had given her about intimacy. The man had obviously used her for his own pleasure without a thought to hers. And, based on what little Diarmid had gleaned from their conversations and the fact that said bastard was notably absent, he left her shortly thereafter. No wonder she struggled to let anyone get close to her.

"I require Diarmid's assistance with a matter of great import," she told Illadan, not so much as glancing at Diarmid. "May I speak with him privately?"

"Of course." Illadan didn't even hesitate. "We were just on our way back to the holding." He motioned for the men to follow as he began the walk back.

Cormac gave Diarmid an encouraging nod before following with the rest of the Fianna. At least one of them believed him capable of handling this.

The moment the men were out of sight, the princess's eyes went straight to his chest. They lingered, taking in every inch of his exposed torso as she walked toward the water's edge. "Help me with one final task, and I swear I will leave you in peace."

Diarmid crossed his arms. "What's the task?"

"I need you to kiss me."

"Absolutely not," he replied. "I have better survival instincts than that."

She rolled her lips, pushing his frayed self-control to its limits. "Sitric said that if I kiss him well enough, he will agree to the betrothal."

"Then kiss *him*," Diarmid suggested, running a hand through his wet hair.

"Oh, no, no, no," Cara protested, storming towards him. "Far too much rests on this for me to make my first attempt with him. If I botch it, that's it. It's over, and we've done all this for naught."

"Are you telling me that bastard that broke your heart bedded you without kissing you?"

Her cheeks went almost as pink as they had when he'd pinned her against the wall.

Almost.

Diarmid threw his shirt to the ground, closing the distance between them.

She didn't back away, didn't even flinch. Not when his hands came up to cup her face and pull her lips to his.

Not when they moved to her hips, pulling her against him so closely that he could hardly breathe.

Not when his teeth nipped at her bottom lip, his tongue teasing her mouth open, until she melted into his arms—just as he'd imagined.

He might not have been her first lover, but damned if he wasn't her first kiss.

Honestly, he was damned either way, so he might as well enjoy it. He squeezed her hips, running his hands over them on their way up her body. God, she felt good in his arms.

She reached for his chest, her fingers leaving a hot trail of pressure over his shoulders. His chest. His stomach. His—

"I wouldn't do that, princess," he warned, not taking his lips off of hers.

Her fingers brushed the tip of him through his trews, though she slowed her exploration at his warning.

A groan escaped his lips before he moved them to her neck,

realizing that he needed to distract her before this got too far. A kiss was one thing.

That was quite another.

Diarmid slid one hand onto her breast, rubbing his thumb over her peaked nipple. He captured her moan of pleasure, returning his lips to hers, kissing her so thoroughly that *this* would be the kiss she always remembered. He was rough. Demanding. Hungry.

He made certain she felt how desperately he wanted her.

He made certain he ruined her for all future kisses.

He didn't stop until both of them were out of breath and their hands couldn't keep from roaming to dangerous places. And when he did finally pull away, he grabbed his shirt off the ground and started walking.

Before he got himself into real trouble.

CHAPTER TWENTY-ONE

PERHAPS, CARA ADMITTED to herself over dinner that eve, kissing Diarmid had been a mistake. She didn't doubt for a moment that it had helped her grow comfortable enough with the act to attempt it with Sitric. No, that part had worked according to plan.

It was everything else that had gone sideways.

That kiss had woken something within her, something that had been stirring since she'd met Diarmid. It had all come back to her as he held her in his arms, as his lips danced with hers. Cara remembered more of the person she'd been before Torna.

It had also piqued her curiosity. Cara had expected the kiss to be as dull as all her previous experiences with intimacy had been. Though Torna had filled her with desire, the moment he'd touched her everything went cold.

She had expected to feel absolutely nothing. Instead, she'd been about ready to take *her own* clothes off. And she'd been devastated when the kiss had ended, leaving her oddly aware of her own body, and the fact that it was no longer pressed against Diarmid's.

Worst of all, Diarmid seemed more determined than usual to avoid her. She promised him that if he helped her with the kiss, she would leave him alone. Apparently, that was what he wanted, though she'd rather hoped not.

She should want Sitric to accept the betrothal. She shouldn't want Diarmid to fight for her, to show any interest in her at all.

Which made it all the more infuriating that she continued to glance his way, hoping for one of those smiles.

After dinner, the servants cleared away the meal and brought out more wine, more ale, and plenty of game boards and knucklebones. Sitric, much like Diarmid, appeared determined to wring as much enjoyment from his life as possible. Though Cara wasn't overly fond of gaming or drinking, she realized that she could learn a thing or two from their habits.

That, and the longer she stayed in the hall, the greater a chance that Diarmid would have to acknowledge her eventually. Cara didn't know precisely what she wanted with him, she just knew that she couldn't lose the first friend she'd made in five years. Not yet.

When she didn't rise to leave for her room, Sitric looked at her askance, smiling. "Are you going to join us?"

"I've not played a game since I was a child," she told him. "I thought it was time to give it another try."

She dared a glance at Diarmid, who still didn't look up.

"I'd suggest knucklebones, then," Sitric said, emptying a small leather bag that sat before them. Five white bones tumbled onto the worn tabletop.

"We take turns trying to play the trick. If you fail, you take a drink. If you succeed, everyone else does. Of course, if you'd rather not drink, I'd be happy to drink your share."

If she was going to play, she was going to do it properly. She'd not had a lick of drink since that night. Surely, one game wouldn't kill her. "I prefer wine, if that's acceptable."

From the corner of her eye, she saw Diarmid's head spin toward her.

"For the first round, you toss them up, then catch them. Like this." Sitric threw the bones and caught all five in his hand, just as he'd instructed, before handing them to Cara. Everyone at the table took a drink.

"It seems to me," Cara observed, ignoring the warm, tingling trickle of the wine down her throat, "that someone with larger hands is at an advantage in this game."

"I'm afraid you're right," Sitric agreed. "And you'll be at a further disadvantage since we've been playing every night," he chuckled.

Cara took the bones from Sitric, testing the weight of them in her hands. There was nothing for it. She tossed them, just as she'd seen Sitric do, and dropped all but one. The table erupted into shouts for her to take a drink, which was oddly comforting in spite of her horrendous failure. She felt a connection to the other players as they laughed and waited their turns.

"You made it look deceptively easy," Cara accused Sitric, taking her second drink of wine in as many turns.

He grinned at her, the same sort of grin she loved when it came from Diarmid. With Sitric, though she was glad he enjoyed himself, it didn't ignite those same desires within her. "Well, I am amazing," he boasted, his tone indicating he jested. Everyone at the table laughed again.

She passed the bones to Astrid beside her, who also completed the trick with no difficulty. As did everyone else around the table.

When they reached Diarmid, Cara's focus naturally went to his hands as he played the trick. But the sight of his hands sent her mind to another place entirely—a riverbank, where those hands squeezed and caressed her, where his lips devoured her. He cupped his hand around the bones, passing them to Cormac as she fought the heat rising within her.

By the third round of the game, Cara realized she'd either need to take Sitric up on his offer or withdraw entirely. The tricks had only gotten more difficult, and Cara had long since accepted that she'd be the one drinking on her turns.

"One more round," Sitric announced, passing her the bones, "then I'm to bed." He reached an arm around Cara's shoulders, setting her on edge. Less so, admittedly, than if she'd not had an entire cup of wine already. Instinctively, she turned toward Diarmid.

He'd been watching, she realized, the muscles in his jaw so tight she could see them working from across the table. His nose flared as he stared at Sitric's arm.

Cara took a deep breath and, instead of ignoring the weight of the arm about her shoulders, she closed her eyes and imagined—nay, remembered—how Diarmid's arms felt wrapped around her only a few hours earlier. When she opened them, she realized everyone stared at her. They couldn't possibly know what she'd been thinking, she assured herself, all the while growing more and more conscious of their unwanted attention.

"It's your turn, *princess*." The word rolled out of his mouth so softly, his voice so rough, Cara could almost feel him whispering it against her skin.

It took her several seconds, after the desire flashed through her and she overcame the shock of him actually speaking to her in public, to realize what he'd said. She looked at the bones before her on the table and picked them up, muttering an apology.

Sitric squeezed her shoulder supportively.

Diarmid looked ready to murder him.

Cara forced herself to stop imagining Diarmid's lips on hers and to focus on taking her turn. Which she failed miserably. She took another sip of wine, passing the bones again to Astrid.

Across from them, Cormac's attention slid from Cara—who hadn't realized he'd been watching her—to Astrid. By the end of the round, Finn was declared the champion for the evening, earning him several bawdy jokes about his dexterous fingers that appeared to deeply upset Dallan.

Niamh rubbed Dallan's shoulders, giggling and whispering something to him that seemed to assuage him. When Niamh noticed Cara watching, she leaned toward her. "Finn is married to his sister," she reminded Cara. "He can be a bit touchy about it, especially when he's in his cups."

Cara had completely forgotten that, though they'd mentioned it several times on their journey to Dyflin. The room cleared, the conversation steadily falling from a roar to a murmur. Sitric bid her goodnight with a sloppy smile, heading for his room. All his warriors and many of the Fianna had departed for their own beds. Cara's face fell when she realized Diarmid had already gone.

CHAPTER TWENTY-TWO

HE HAD TO get out of that hall. Sitric was his friend, a man he truly respected, whose company he enjoyed more than most. Yet it was all he could do to keep from leaping over the table and ripping his arm off of Cara. And punching him in the face while he was at it.

Worse, Diarmid knew it was Sitric's arm, not his own, that actually belonged there.

"Where are we going?" his brother Conan asked, hurrying to catch up with Diarmid as he stormed down the hill and away from Sitric's holding.

"Diarmid needs a night out," Cormac answered for him, appearing on his other side.

"Diarmid needs a good fight," Diarmid grumbled at his brothers.

"I'll fight you," Conan offered cheerily. "I never tire of beating your sorry arse."

They'd made it halfway down the hill, the first houses as far before them as Sitric's lay behind, when Cormac pulled Diarmid to a halt.

"It's better to let it out," Cormac advised. "No judgment here. Right, Conan?"

Conan looked like he might make another jest, until he saw Diarmid's face. "Right," he agreed. "What am I missing? I feel like you both know something I don't."

Cormac shot Diarmid a pointed look. "Let it out."

"I can't stop thinking about her." Diarmid pinched the bridge of his nose. "I have to stop helping her. I can't take it any longer."

"Maybe I can help her instead," Conan offered. "Are you just talking with her?"

"He's not," Cormac said.

Conan's eyes went wide. "You're not bedding her, are you? Sitric will—"

"I'm not."

"What happened at the river today?" Cormac asked as he resumed their journey to The Broken Oar.

"What makes you think anything happened?" Diarmid shot back. "I said the same thing to you days ago."

Cormac nodded. "Aye, you did. But this morning, the princess hardly spared you a glance. At dinner, she couldn't take her eyes off you. You should talk to her about that, by the way. If Sitric sees the way she's looking at you, he's going to figure it out."

"I'm not talking to her again," Diarmid replied.

Conan furrowed his brow. "Figure out *what*?"

Diarmid couldn't bring himself to say it aloud. What had happened to him? Where had the man gone who bedded a different woman each night?

Cormac shoved him. Hard.

"Fine!" Diarmid cried. "It's possible that I've grown fond of her."

"Good God." Conan put a hand to Diarmid's forehead. "Have you caught an ague? Have the fair folk gotten you? You wandered into one of their forts, didn't you?"

Diarmid swatted his hand away. "I'm fine."

"You didn't smile once the entire night," Cormac observed.

"You want me to smile as I watch him put his hands all over her?" The words came out before Diarmid realized what he'd said.

"Are you sure you haven't bedded her?" Conan's skepticism was entirely merited.

At least Diarmid hadn't been that foolish.

Cormac cast him a sideways glance. "Have you?"

"I already told you I haven't," Diarmid replied testily. He could tell by the looks on their faces that they still didn't believe him. "She made me kiss her."

Conan let out an irritating laugh. "You jest."

"No judgment." Cormac's clipped reminder had Conan sobering quickly. "Go on, Diarmid. Ignore this fool, I'm genuinely curious."

"I've been helping her grow more accustomed to physical touch. Not like that, you arse," he growled when a strangled chuckle escaped Conan. "Sitric hugs everyone. He tried several times to hold her hand and she struggled to accommodate him. So, I sat and held her hand until she deemed it tolerable."

"I did notice she'd improved with that," Conan told him. "Whatever you did, it's working."

"So what happened today, then?" Cormac pressed.

"Sitric told her if she kissed him, he'd marry her. More or less." Diarmid ran a hand through his hair as he recalled their conversation. "She'd never kissed anyone before, and begged me to help her this last time."

Both his brothers were silent until they'd nearly reached the alehouse. "You need to bed someone," Cormac insisted yet again. "It's always worked for you in the past, and it makes the most sense for this particular problem."

"I tried! Don't you remember? The serving maid?"

"Maybe she wasn't the right woman—"

"When have you *ever* known me to be selective over women with breasts that size?"

"I bet they bounce nicely," Conan added unhelpfully. "Perhaps you should go give her another try."

Cormac moved in front of Diarmid, placing both hands on his shoulders. "Four days. One raid. Then you never have to see her again. I know that's not what you want, but it will be easier to move on when she isn't sitting across from you at every meal."

"Speaking of which," Conan said, "what's going on with you and Astrid?"

"I loathe her almost as much as she loathes me," Cormac replied, sounding irritated for the first time the entire night. "My deepest wish is to leave this settlement before she tries to kill me in my sleep."

Conan wiggled his eyebrows at Diarmid with a knowing glance, earning a glower from Cormac. Diarmid had to admit that it was rare indeed to see his eldest brother so easily riled, or to have him say anything that appeared unfounded.

Conan continued teasing Cormac as they sat at a table outside, waiting for Maeve to bring their drinks. They spoke of the raid with Sitric, of the Fianna, even of their childhood and their shared disgust of their father, who had turned his back on Brian after years as an ally. For a time, Diarmid nearly forgot all about his troubles with Cara.

Cormac was right. All Diarmid needed to do was get through the next few days. Once they returned home, he wouldn't have to see Cara again.

If only that was what he wanted.

Instead, he wanted to learn about her childhood. He wanted to learn the name of whatever bastard had used her so poorly so he could hunt him down. He wanted to know what she thought about Dyflin, about her family's problems, about her own capture and rescue. As he sat under the twinkling stars with his brothers, letting the chill night air clear his mind, Diarmid realized that though he'd loved every woman he'd bedded, he'd not once fallen *in* love.

Until now.

CHAPTER TWENTY-THREE

THE SOONER SHE kissed him, the sooner she'd be through this nightmare, Cara told herself. Niamh combed Cara's hair—something they did several times a day while she wore it down in an effort to win over Sitric. Unfortunately, Diarmid appeared correct, and Sitric warmed to her considerably when she left it loose.

All she had to do was kiss him. Kissing Diarmid had been easy. And pleasant. So pleasant that she found she couldn't dwell on the memory for long or she'd lose all nerve to continue with Sitric.

"How did you know you loved Dallan?" Cara asked as Niamh worked through the multitude of tangles.

Niamh thought for a moment, looking wistful. "He always makes me feel good about myself," she said at last. "When I'm with him, I feel as though I could do anything. And he makes me laugh," she added with a grin. "He's always there for me, even when I'm at my worst, and I try to do the same for him."

Diarmid had been there for her since the moment she'd met him. He'd seen her at her worst—when she was so broken by Torna that she could hardly bear to be near anyone—and had helped her until she began to heal.

"It takes time," Niamh continued when Cara sat in silence. "You've only just met Sitric."

If only she'd been asking about Sitric. "How long did it take for you to know you loved Dallan?"

Niamh bit her lip, tossing a long, golden braid over her shoulder as she moved to comb the front portion of Cara's tresses. "Well, that's a bit different. I was young, and he was my first love—"

"How long?"

"About a day," Niamh sighed. "But it took seven years for us to make it work, even knowing we loved each other."

A day seemed short, even to Cara, and seven years—interminable. "But you knew the day you met him?"

"I did," she admitted. "But most people don't. Finn courted Eva for months before they realized they were in love."

"Isn't Illadan married as well?" Cara thought she remembered him mentioning his wife over dinner the other day.

Niamh chuckled. "To Finn's little sister, aye."

Cara turned to her wide-eyed. "No," she breathed conspiratorially.

"Yes." Niamh nodded. "And she's carrying already. You should have seen Finn's face when he found out."

"About the marriage or the babe?"

"Both," she laughed. "He's usually a gentle soul, but I thought he might attack Illadan. There," she declared, setting the comb on a small bedside table, "all finished."

Cara thanked her, standing and stretching. Walking out of her room and into the main hall, she found Sitric waiting for her. They'd been meeting most mornings, going on walks about his holding and the town in an attempt to grow acquainted. Cara certainly felt that she knew Sitric better, but he still never brought flutters to her stomach or made her heart race.

Not like Diarmid.

Every time she saw Sitric, every time he grabbed her hand or hugged her, Cara could hear Diarmid's clandestine confession. Feel his hands on her hips, so big that his fingers nearly touched over her stomach. Taste his mouth against hers.

Maybe that's what it would be like with Sitric as well. She'd only ever kissed Diarmid. For all Cara knew, kisses were much the same no matter the people involved.

"Ready?" Sitric asked, taking her hand. "I've somewhere to show you that I think you'll find enchanting."

They walked the way they always went, out of Sitric's holding and down the road leading into the heart of Dyflin. Countless houses came and went, the ship masts rising to their right in a harbor hidden from view. Children ran laughing through the buildings and along the roadways. Sitric was oddly quiet, not asking any questions as he usually did. He stopped outside a hall marked as a metalsmith's shop, opening the door for Cara and following her inside.

Two guards stood at the door, nodding to Sitric as they passed. She expected a blast of heat, thinking there would be a smith's forge running somewhere inside. Instead, she found a window-lined hall, filled with trestle tables where men sat on stools bent over their work. Scattered over the table were bowls and bins filled with bits of metal, small tools, and more gemstones than Cara had seen in one place.

"Well that explains the guards," she said.

"Indeed," Sitric agreed. "Though we have very few attempts at thievery."

A small fire burned in the center of the hall, but nothing like a billowing forge. Several craftsmen waved and greeted Sitric, who took Cara's hand to wander down the first row of tables.

"This is where they design jewelry, brooches, inlaid belts, bowls, hilts," Sitric explained, gesturing to many of the items as they appeared on the tables. "Anything that requires finesse and sparkles enough to tempt a dragon, they craft here."

Cara inspected a large cross, crafted of gold and inlaid with rubies, that a man was polishing. "They're beautiful," she told him. "It must require a great deal of training to make such fine designs."

"It does indeed. And this is where craftsmen from all over the island come to do just that." He looked over her shoulder at the golden cross. "You favor that one?"

She jumped back, hitting his chest before stepping to the side. "No," she replied. "I mean, yes, it's beautiful, but—"

"Which one do you like, then?"

Cara's stomach swirled into a knot tighter than any sailor could render. "They're all beautiful," she hedged, sensing now the purpose of the excursion.

"So I should buy them all?" His grin was full of mischief and charm.

But he wasn't Diarmid.

In that moment, Cara realized he never would be. "You deserve someone who will smile with you," she said softly.

He took her hand, pulling her away from the tables. "And you deserve someone who will make you smile," he replied. "That you even would say such a thing tells me there is hope for this betrothal yet. Perhaps in time I'll see you laugh."

"Even before—" she began, catching herself. "I've never been much given to laughter and smiles. My mother always chastised me for my serious manner, even when I was small."

"You're still small," he teased. She certainly was compared with Sitric. And with Diarmid. "And though appreciated, laughter is not required." His hand rose to her ear, tucking a strand of hair behind it tenderly.

Cara imagined Diarmid doing the same, and instantly felt less like cringing—though infinitely more guilty. Sitric deserved a woman who craved his touch as she did Diarmid's. He was too kind to be wasted on her.

"I've grown fond of you and your strange habits this past sennight," he continued. "I wish to give you a gift, to celebrate our impending betrothal."

"But I haven't—" she paused, not wanting to speak of such intimate things with fifty other men within earshot.

His hand moved to her face, cradling it as Diarmid had when he'd come to her room at midnight. Before he'd pinned her against the wall and made her want him so badly she still hadn't stopped.

"I know," Sitric whispered. "But you will."

CHAPTER TWENTY-FOUR

DIARMID FELT BOTH better and worse after the night out with his brothers. It had been cathartic to speak with them about Cara. Hearing their reassurance that his growing feelings would pass with time, if he could only manage a few more days, took away some of his worries. But it did nothing to ease the growing ache in his heart as he realized the only woman he'd ever truly loved was going to marry another man.

He entered the guest hall with the other Fianna, freshly washed and returning his muck-covered clothes to the box in his room. He sincerely hoped Sitric paid the launderer an enormous bonus for all the extra washing the Fianna generated. Perhaps he ought to mention that to Illadan, in the hopes the guilt of it might finally end their runs through the bog.

As the men dispersed to their rooms to wait for dinner, Diarmid halted before his own door.

It was closed.

He'd left it open. He looked about to see if Conan or Dallan had set some sort of trick for him, but both of them had already gone. Deciding that perhaps the launderer or maid had closed it on her way out, Diarmid opened the door.

Nothing seemed amiss, so he shut it behind him, thinking to lie down until the bell rang for dinner. Before he'd taken two steps, Cara popped out from the other side of his bed, where she'd clearly been crouching.

"I couldn't risk just anyone walking in and finding me here," she explained when he frowned at her. "And I knew you'd not agree to meet me again."

"Whatever this is," Diarmid told her, "it's a terrible idea."

"Sitric as good as agreed to the betrothal today," she said, sitting on his bed. As though the image of her anywhere near his bed didn't drive him mad.

"I do *not* want all the sordid details of you kissing some other man."

"I didn't kiss him."

"Then how did you get him to agree?"

"He didn't agree, exactly." Her tongue darted out to lick her bottom lip, forcing Diarmid to move farther away from the temptress. "I felt so badly that all I could think about was you, that I told him he deserved someone who would smile with him. And then he said he expected that we would be getting betrothed."

"Wait." Diarmid ran a hand down his face. "You tried to tell him that you shouldn't marry at all, and he decided that meant it would work?"

"Yes."

Then her words sank in. Diarmid moved slowly back toward the bed. "You tried to refuse the betrothal?"

"He's a kind man," she replied. "I don't want him to spend his life married to someone who doesn't want him."

Diarmid's heart pounded against his chest as he neared her. He should end this now. Before he destroyed the alliance. Before he put her family at risk. Instead, he asked, "Who do you want, princess?"

Her eyes went cloudy, her breath heavy. "You."

He should tell her they both had responsibilities, people who were counting on them. He should do anything except throw her down on that bed beneath him.

And yet, somehow, that's exactly what he did.

His mouth crashed over hers again, his hands sliding with insistent pressure up her body to cup her breasts. Last time, his kiss had made her melt. This time, it set her on fire. She arched into his touch, wondering when she'd cease enjoying the feel of him above her.

That thought seized her, and she remembered being stuck beneath Torna—uncomfortable and in a good deal of pain once he'd entered her.

Diarmid stilled atop her, his eyes searching her face. "Are you alright?"

She swallowed down some of the panic. Diarmid was nothing like Torna. "I just recalled the last time I was in this position," she whispered, mortified at her confession, "and it wasn't a terribly pleasant experience. Torna—"

"I'm going to stop you right there, princess." His husky voice stirred those butterflies right up. "First, that bastard has no idea how to pleasure a woman, as I'm about to show you." His soft lips laid a trail of kisses from her forehead to her neck, his hands circling her nipples, sending a buzzing sensation straight to her core.

"And second?" she managed, her hands reaching for his broad shoulders.

"*Never* say another man's name while you're in my bed," he growled. "Agreed?"

She nodded. "So, it won't hurt?"

His wicked grin lit up her world, his eyes sparkling with mischief in their shared moment. "No," his voice broke. "It won't hurt."

She took his stubbly face in her hands, the short hairs tickling her fingers as she pulled him back for another kiss. His hands unlaced her gown with expert swiftness, a fact she chose not to dwell upon. When he'd laid her bare, he pulled away, his hooded gaze raking over her lustfully.

Then he devoured her.

His mouth went to her breasts, his teeth gently tugging on one, stiffened nipple before bathing it with a wet kiss. Nothing she'd ever done with Torna had felt this incredible, had filled her with such aching desire—an ache that now pooled at the center of her legs.

As though reading her thoughts, Diarmid's lips moved down the delicate skin of her belly. His fingers brushed the very place where she burned for him, teasing her. A soft moan escaped her as he massaged that sensitive area between her legs. She felt his smile against her skin, could see it in her mind's eye.

He pressed a hot kiss to her hip before she felt him *there*. She was ready to sit up and protest, when he started sucking on her. Instead of a protest, she let out an oath that made him chuckle, the vibration of it only intensifying the pressure building within her.

Diarmid lifted himself up onto his forearms, looking like an absolute rogue. His wild, dark hair fell to his muscular shoulders in disarray, his gaze so hot it might have burned her. "You're going to have to be quieter than that, princess."

Cara was thoroughly ruined, she realized as she savored the rough sound of his voice. She'd only ever been in bed with two men, and there was no comparison to be made. She doubted there ever would be.

She gasped as his mouth returned to her, licking and sucking as his fingers slipped inside of her. The sensations that had plagued her every time she was close to him, the ache, the burning, the mounting pressure somewhere inside her built up until she was certain she would burst into pieces.

"Diarmid," she cried, unable to comprehend what was happening. Just when she wondered when his sweet torment would end, she did burst, in a way she couldn't even put to words. It was as though the whole world fell away, taking her with it, and when she opened her eyes an extraordinary sense of calm descended.

Then the dinner bell rang.

"I like the sound of my name on your lips," he said, helping her up off the bed.

"What happened?" she asked.

That cheeky grin reappeared. "What's supposed to happen every time you lay with someone."

He helped her back into her shift and gown, turning her about so he could lace it for her.

"It happens to men as well?" Cara struggled to wrap her mind around this entirely new experience. "Did you feel it as well?"

"It does happen to men, at the end," he explained. "This time I wanted to focus on you."

"So you could have had it happen, but you didn't? Did I do something wrong?"

He placed his hands on her shoulders, locking their eyes. "You did nothing wrong. We would have had to do a whole lot more than that for it to happen to me, which is something I'm more than willing to explore later."

"Why later?" That had been so incredible, she felt it only right that Diarmid should share in it with her.

"Because if we don't get to the hall for dinner, you'll get to explain what we just did to everyone else."

The dinner bell. She'd utterly ignored it. Letting out another oath, Cara hurried ahead of him to the main hall.

And the man who believed they'd be getting married.

CHAPTER TWENTY-FIVE

HE WAS GOING straight to hell.

And it was absolutely worth it.

Diarmid struggled through the meal, unable to think of anything except the way Cara tasted on his lips, so sweet and feminine.

The way she sounded as she cried out his name while he pleasured her.

The way she felt as she came apart in his arms.

Oh, he was going to hell alright. But he'd be grinning like a fool on his way there.

Cara made a point of looking everywhere but at Diarmid. He knew this because, God help him, he couldn't take his eyes off her. He'd been with more women than he cared to count, and not one of them had captured him so completely. Though they'd all been enjoyable, not a single one had been unforgettable. But he hadn't even bedded Cara and he knew he'd never forget her.

Cormac spoke to her, forcing her to look in Diarmid's direction. Her eyes went to him only briefly, but it was enough to send streaks of pink bursting to her cheeks. No doubt because her mind strayed to the same place his had been residing.

They agreed to meet before everyone left the hall, since fewer people would be milling about outside while the games were happening. After eating only a portion of her plate, Cara excused herself, retreating to her room. When dinner was finished, Diarmid admitted to being too tired for games that night, leaving the hall and sneaking to Cara's window to help her out of it.

They rushed through the narrow patch of grass separating the halls, the light long gone now that they'd entered the dark half of the year. With her hand held tightly in his, Diarmid threw open the back door to the guest hall.

To find Finn standing just inside the front entrance, staring straight at them. Finn shut the door behind him, crossing his arms over his chest. "Well," he sighed, "I certainly wish I'd remembered my harp." He strode over to the hearth in the center of the room, waiting. "Diarmid, a word?"

Cara dropped Diarmid's hand like it had caught fire, all but running to his room and shutting the door. A sinking feeling settled into the pit of Diarmid's stomach as he joined Finn near the hearth.

"I don't want to know the details," Finn began, "and I'm not going to even ask if you've lost the wager, because you're buying me a drink either way. But I am going to need you to tell me what the hell is going on, since I swore to Brian that the woman in your bedroom would marry Sitric."

Seeing no way around it, at Finn's insistence Diarmid told him the entire tale, from the day they'd arrived in Dyflin. Leaving out, also at Finn's insistence, all of the intimate details.

Finn fell into a chair beside the glittering embers. "As it happens, I know a thing or two about sneaking around with a woman, and I'm going to give you some advice whether you want it or not."

Diarmid thought that entirely fair, given the situation. "Please." He sat in the fur-laden chair across from Finn.

"You need to decide what this really is," Finn told him. "Are you in love with her? Is she in love with you? Are you starved for companionship and using this obsession to compensate? You need to discuss this with Cara and be brutally honest. Because if you really do love each other, and she refuses to marry Sitric, then you need to go tell him you've been bedding her."

"I haven't been—"

"Close enough," Finn interrupted. "But trust me when I tell you, the very worst thing in this situation would be for Sitric to find out from anyone other than you. As uncomfortable as you imagine that discussion may be, anything else will be catastrophic, and not just for you."

Diarmid remembered what happened when Dallan discovered that Finn had been sneaking around with his sister. Everyone did. It had nearly destroyed their friendship. For a time, Diarmid believed that it had.

"I wish that it were just an obsession," Diarmid admitted quietly.

"But you love her."

Diarmid let out a breath. "I don't want to ruin this entire mission. And I consider Sitric a friend, odd though that may seem."

"If you value his friendship, confront him about this. If he's a true friend, he'll understand. He may punch you in the face," Finn added with a wry smile, "but he'll come around eventually."

"What of Brian?" Diarmid asked. It was the one question he'd not dared to pose even to himself, not until he had no choice but to consider it.

Finn shrugged. "I couldn't begin to guess. He's always been a bit of a romantic, but he's a shrewd politician. If you go through with this, you need to decide how much you're willing to give up for her. Will you risk losing your place among the Fianna? Will she risk losing her land and title?"

It struck Diarmid then that no matter what decision he made, he would be disappointing someone. Yet again.

"Don't do what I did," Finn advised, rising and placing a hand on Diarmid's shoulder. "Be prepared for the consequences before you take the action."

"Thank you," Diarmid called as Finn hurried to get the harp from his room. "Truly, I appreciate it."

"You owe me a drink tomorrow," Finn reminded him on his way out of the hall.

Diarmid owed his friend a lot more than a drink. He stood there alone, staring into the dying embers of the hearth, collecting his thoughts. In the distance, cheers erupted as an expertly plied harp filled the night with a heartrending tune. As Finn's strong, steady voice took up the melody, Diarmid made his decision.

He walked toward his room, gathering his courage for the conversation that awaited him.

CHAPTER TWENTY-SIX

CARA PACED THE confines of Diarmid's room. Waiting.

She hated waiting.

She didn't know Finn terribly well, but he seemed a decent enough fellow not to overreact. Honestly, Cara worried more over Diarmid than herself. She knew that the Fianna were his family and it would destroy him to let them down. Cara didn't envy him the conversation he was having with Finn right now, and she felt more than a little responsible for it.

Diarmid's room, and all the rooms that adjoined the halls, were nearly identical. Wattle mats covered the floors, always clean and smooth. Each held a bed, covered in woolen blankets and at least one fur—a testament to Sitric's immense wealth. A small table, a chest to store belongings, a washing stand with a bowl, and a brazier filled what remained of the modest space. Cozy and minimal, Sitric's halls put most others to shame with their accommodations.

The floor creaked as Cara turned on her heels once again and paced the other direction at the foot of the bed. She had no way of gauging how long she waited. Every moment felt like an eternity. When the door finally opened, she turned expectantly, her heart racing.

Diarmid's face was so serious—more so than she'd ever seen him. It made her realize how much she missed the man who teased her and laughed all day long, who had once irritated her endlessly. Right now, she'd give anything to have him back, shameless flirting and all.

"This is my fault," she said as he shut the door behind him.

He stared at her, silent but not upset. At least not that she could sense. His chestnut eyes blazed, strong and determined. She knew that whatever he said, it was final, a decision he'd reached after great thought.

Cara had every intention of waiting for him to finally speak, but not knowing what he thought, caught in the stillness hovering between them, she could bear it no longer. "I'm so sorry," she whispered.

When she had nearly given up, preparing to leave him to his own thoughts until he was ready, he finally spoke—the last words she'd expected to hear.

"I love you." He didn't move, didn't flinch or take a single step as he watched for her reaction. "I've tried not to, as it would make all of this infinitely easier. But I don't think it's within my control."

Cara's head spun as she digested his words. Caught unawares, she found herself facing the very question she'd posed to Niamh earlier that morn. When would she know that she was in love?

More importantly, did she want to be in love? She'd believed that Torna had loved her, he'd even said as much. And look where it had gotten her.

He took a step toward her. "Finn suggested that, if we are serious about this, we should tell Sitric."

Cara sat on the foot of the bed, wringing her clammy hands together, her mind racing. She felt so many things. She thought so many things. And none of it made sense to her, not one thought or feeling produced anything she could offer up to Diarmid in response.

Another step forward, his gaze unwavering. "I'm prepared to leave, to let you proceed with the betrothal, if that's what you wish. But I'm also prepared to risk everything for you."

Her stomach roiled in protest at facing such a decision so soon. She tried taking a deep breath but found her lungs uncooperative. Pressing her hand against her heaving chest, she forced herself to focus.

"I don't want to marry Sitric." It was the first thing Cara could put to words, the first full idea after the storm of emotion his statement had caused within her.

Diarmid nodded. "Then we should tell him that."

"I need more than a fortnight to decide to marry someone," she said at last, painfully aware that it wasn't what he wanted to hear.

"To marry someone outside of duty, you mean." She heard the way he tried to hide the hurt in his voice.

Cara took a shaky breath. "That was different," she whispered. "You, of all people, know that." She thought he'd been the only one who saw Torna for what he truly was, the first one to tell her she hadn't made the mistake—Torna had. He closed the final steps between them. "And you, of all people, know that I'm not him." He lifted his hand to her cheek, caressing it tenderly. "Do you want me to leave?"

"No," she breathed, soaking in the warmth of his skin against hers. "I want more time with you before I decide anything. I want you, but it's all so much, so quickly."

And she'd wanted Torna, too. Or thought she had. And she'd known him for months, had spoken with him countless times, courted him properly. Only to discover that she hadn't truly known him at all.

Diarmid was different, aye, but she wasn't about to dive in too quickly again. After all, he'd never wanted a marriage as far as she could tell—just a string of women he left behind as he carved a path of bedmates across Éire. Cara knew him well enough to realize she was more than that to him—but how much more? Could she really trust him not to leave her as well?

His deep, dark eyes searched her face. "You doubt me," he said.

"I hardly know you," she replied. "Until this past fortnight, I knew you as a rogue who took a different woman to bed each night and knew nothing of responsibility. I know you better than that now, but not much." She took his hand off her cheek and held it tightly. "Give me a little more time, stay with me, just as you have been, and I will be ready."

His soft smile tore at her heart. "I've not bedded a woman since we rescued you."

Had he cared for her even then? Had he truly abstained from his indulgences even before they grew closer? No wonder he seemed so different now—he had changed entirely. "I will tell Sitric in the morn," she promised, hoping such a final act would show him she meant it.

Diarmid shook his head. "You can't tell him right before we leave for battle," he replied. "I will tell him after the raid, so it doesn't distract him."

"Diarmid, I should be the one to do it."

"He was my friend before he was promised to you," Diarmid insisted. "Please, let me speak with him."

Cara nodded her agreement. It was the least she could do since she'd no doubt wounded him with her cold response.

He leaned forward, his lips brushing hers. The kiss felt like a warm summer day, unhurried, soaked in sunshine, and full of promise. His soft, insistent pressure against her mouth left her with no doubts as to his intentions.

Come battles or betrothals, Diarmid meant to stay.

And for Cara, that was enough.

CHAPTER TWENTY-SEVEN

TWO DAYS LATER, Cara sat upon a mossy bank by the harbor, watching as the Fianna and Sitric's men practiced their rowing drills once more. She'd come to watch them the first day as well, which had been plenty entertaining as they learned to row a longship. Many of the Fianna had similar features, particularly as many were related in one way or another, making them difficult to distinguish from such a distance.

Finn stood out instantly near the bow of the ship, grinning like a fool as a wave broke over the bow and covered him in its salty mist. His blonde hair matched the sun-bleached gangways that jutted into the bay, making him the easiest to spot. He'd been in the best mood Cara had seen since she'd met him when he learned they would be training for a *viking*.

The rest of the men had the wild, dark hair so prevalent amongst the native people and shared a similar size and build. Unsurprising, as they'd all managed to perform the same feats of strength and skill to become Fianna in the first place. Squinting against the glare of the midmorning sun, Cara finally identified Diarmid when he stood to change posts with someone.

Diarmid had not been himself since their discussion. He didn't make jokes or laugh. He'd kissed her plenty, and then some, but it felt—different. As though he held back something that he hadn't before. Cara knew something was wrong. And she knew it had to do with her.

A frigid breeze blew across the sea, puckering the colorful

sails that filled the harbor. Cara pulled the wolfskin cloak that Sitric had let her borrow tighter about her shoulders. Though the sun beat down—a rare occurrence in Dyflin, Sitric had told her—midwinter fast approached, and the weather had a biting chill that crept further in from the edges of each day.

As the longship rushed across the waters toward the horizon, Cara recalled the tales of the Myrmidons, led by the fearless Achilles. She wished the men before her the same prowess in battle as those mighty warriors of old. They'd always captured her imagination, these great kings and warriors and their tales of adventure and battle. Though she'd seen many a warrior in her father's army, nothing brought to mind her beloved stories like watching the Fianna train.

"Magnificent, isn't it?" Sitric plopped down onto the ground beside her, his arms resting on his bent knees. "Astrid complains of the smell of the harbor, but all I see are blue skies and opportunity."

"The wind makes certain that you mainly smell the sea anyway," Cara replied, breathing deeply of the briny breeze. Then, unable to contain her curiosity, she asked, "Why opportunity?" It seemed an odd choice of words.

"Because you could meet anyone here," he explained. "You could see anything, learn anything. It provides an opportunity to expand both my kingdom's wealth and my understanding of the world." He pointed at a large cargo ship grounded on the far side of the harbor. "That cog is captained by a man who speaks fifteen languages. Fifteen. I've made a point of speaking with him every time he makes it back this way, solely to hear the stories he tells."

"Where is he from?"

Sitric chuckled. "He made me swear I'd never tell anyone, since I butcher the language so badly. I can't say he's wrong. But he tells me that where he comes from there are serpents as long as two tall men that can swallow a deer whole."

Cara's eyes went wide. "What!"

"I know!" Sitric shivered in a mockery of fear. "And cats as large as a man, covered in orange and black stripes that prowl through the forests. He's been to places that I couldn't have imagined in my dreams."

They sat in companionable silence for a time, Cara alternately watching the longship as it turned about back toward the harbor and contemplating a place where such creatures as Sitric described might exist. It was the first time she'd felt truly comfortable in his presence, Cara realized.

"I wanted to speak with you about the betrothal," Sitric ventured as the Fianna's ship neared the shallows.

Cara looked over to him, his pale hair streaked with auburn—the only nod to his mother's fiery locks. Guilt stabbed at her gut. She hadn't given a thought to the terms he'd delivered—a kiss for a betrothal. Lord, what if he meant to kiss her right now?

She glanced at the longship, just approaching the shoreline and preparing to land. Diarmid had wanted to tell Sitric after the raid, worried his friend would be too distracted otherwise. How could she put him off without making a denial outright?

And then there were the political ramifications to consider, which they had only briefly discussed. Was Cara prepared to give up her land and title, her sister's home, and possibly the last shreds of her family's reputation for Diarmid? He felt so distant these past days, perhaps he regretted it already.

What if she refused Sitric only to have Diarmid decide she wasn't worth the trouble?

"I have given it much thought since our last discussion," Sitric began, "and I will agree to a betrothal as Brian has asked."

Cara swallowed. "What of the kiss?"

Sitric grinned. "By all means, offer it if you wish. But after spending more time together, I don't think it would be as miserable as I once believed."

"May I ask why?"

"In part, I feel that you are finally showing more of yourself as the days pass. And though we are quite different, we have more in common than I thought." He paused to gauge her reaction before continuing. "Mainly, if I'm honest, it's that the lure of land in Mumhain is terribly tempting. We have some farms here, in the countryside outside the settlement, and they send us what they can. But we spend a good deal of coin importing crops that we could grow in your kingdom far better."

Cara appreciated the blunt honesty in his words. "The countryside there is dotted with a patchwork of productive farms," Cara agreed, her nerves gaining ground. Of course, he decided the marriage based upon what was best for his kingdom. That he'd even take his personal feelings into account at all should have struck her as odd. "I imagine it would be beneficial to you as well to hold land within Brian's kingdom."

Sitric looked at his hands. "I suppose that sounds terribly heartless, doesn't it? That my final decision came from political gain?"

"On the contrary," Cara replied. "It sounds much more like you're a wise king who puts his people before himself."

"I try to be, on occasion." He offered her a playful half-smile. "But I never forget that I am also a man, else how can I relate to my people?"

She wished, more than anything, that she could tell him the truth in this moment. He spoke in measured tones of things that truly mattered to him. If there were a time to offer him the truth, this was it.

But Cara had promised Diarmid that he could be the one to broach the topic with his friend. She understood now, even more than she had when she'd seen them partake in companionable revelry, how they'd become friends.

"What say you?" he asked when she made no reply. "Shall we have the contract drawn up before I go?"

"Could we wait until your return?" Cara schooled her features into the same neutral look she'd worn much of her life.

He raised a brow. "What's this? The woman who's been doing everything in her power to convince me to marry her now hesitates?" His voice held no censure, only curiosity and bemusement, a lightness she knew never came from her own lips.

"It's just that I was expecting another few days before you agreed," she hurried—and it wasn't entirely fabricated, either. "I'm surprised, is all."

"Well, in that case why don't we wait until I return from the raid," he offered. "It will give you the few days you'd expected, and I will focus on preparing for battle instead of drawing up a contract."

"That would be lovely," she agreed. "Thank you."

He stood, smiling at her. "Excellent. We'll discuss the details when I return."

Cara rose with him, collecting her blanket and walking back toward Sitric's holding by his side, trying not to let her guilt eat her up along the way.

CHAPTER TWENTY-EIGHT

THE HALLS THRUMMED with life. Sitric's entire holding was filled to bursting with every fighting man who could squeeze a space for himself in the revelry. As always, the meal began in the midafternoon and lasted until near sunset. But folk arrived early and stayed long into the night, setting up contests of strength and wit and drink wherever space could be found.

The meal itself—a grand display of meats, sweets, and root vegetables that would have impressed any king—passed quickly, with minimal conversation. Every man there had spent the better part of the past two days rowing a longship or sparring in the fields. Ravenous was too weak a word for the hunger that consumed them.

Typically, Sitric would have called in a skald to play music and tell stories as entertainment after the feast. But, as he'd pointed out, he currently hosted an entire unit of skalds, since all Fianna had to learn to play the harp and perform the poems and histories of Éire. Finn and Ardál, the two most gifted bards among the Fianna, volunteered for the task.

Diarmid managed to get a seat beside Cara. It had become something of a custom, where each of them sat at the meals when all were present. But the tables were moved to make space for dancing and sport, and everyone who wanted to game had to relocate to the edges of the room where the tables had gone.

Palpable tension—and not the sort that led to Diarmid's favorite recreational activity—filled their shared moments. It was his fault. He didn't know what he'd expected when he went into that room and poured out his heart, but he realized now he shouldn't have expected the same from Cara.

Had that not been the crux of their relationship? That she had such trouble with intimacy that she needed his help to take even the smallest of steps? Diarmid should have known admitting to something so emotional as love would take her more than a fortnight. He had years of experience to compare against his present situation, to contrast starkly the fleeting emotions he'd had for other women and the all-encompassing yearning he had for Cara. Yet, even armed with this understanding, her rejection had stung.

Tonight, he meant to make it up to her. He'd been feeling rather sorry for himself, even wondering if he'd made a mistake in taking such a risk with so much unknown, and he saw it reflected back at him in the return of her chilly demeanor.

And he simply couldn't have that.

So he sat beside her, earning a scandalized look when he squeezed her thigh in the chaos of the seat shuffling. With a quick wink, he moved his attention to their gaming companions. It was a test of will not to turn back and see her reaction.

Sitric, Dallan, Cormac, and Conan joined them at one of the long trestle tables, drinks and knucklebones in hand. Sitric also carried his bag of runes, taking a seat on the other side of Cara from Diarmid. The other three took the bench across from them.

Finn began a dancing tune on the harp, Ardál striking up a harmony shortly thereafter. Spirits waxed as the night rode on past dusk.

"Shall we cast the runes?" Sitric asked. Though, Diarmid mused, the Ostman king knew full well none would oppose him in his own home. Or at all, really, as the practice didn't bother any of the Fianna. Brian still employed a druid as one of his advisors, as had been recommended for generations untold. He had a priest as well, of course, but every good king listened to them both.

"Should we drink before or after casting them?" Diarmid asked.

Sitric laughed. "For me after. For you, both."

Diarmid raised his mug. "As the king commands." Dallan, Conan, and even Cormac also raised their mugs and drank deeply with him. Cara hadn't taken a sip since they sat down.

Sitric opened the leather pouch that held his runes. He gave it a good shake before dumping the smooth, wooden pieces onto the table, inspecting them with narrowed eyes.

"Well?" Dallan demanded. "Is it awful?"

"We aren't truly going to cancel the raid just because of a drunken rune casting," Cormac said, leveling him a look.

"Oh, no, we would," Sitric countered, deadly serious. "But fortunately, we won't need to." He stood, turning toward the center of the hall. "The runes say we sail at dawn!" he shouted, rousing the room to a raucous cheer.

Everyone in sight—except Cara—grabbed the nearest drink, cheering once more before settling back to their previous endeavors. Sitric sat again, turning to his companions. "Are you ready for two days of rowing?"

Diarmid grinned. "I should ask the same of you. We've been training, but I worry you'll be so out of condition after lounging in your halls all day that your ship won't be able to keep up with ours."

Sitric leaned over the table, eyes narrowed, his lip doing its damndest to repress a smile. "Is that a challenge?"

"Only if there's silver on the line," Diarmid shot back.

"There could be."

"Five silver pieces to whoever lands first at Cill Cliethe," Conan said, all too eager to join in the fun.

"You've got yourself a wager," Sitric agreed, sitting back and taking a long drink of ale.

"You seem to be accumulating those, Diarmid," Dallan chuckled.

He wasn't wrong. "You've got to find the fun in life," Diarmid responded.

"I couldn't agree more." Sitric raised his horn in approval. "What other wagers have you? I feel I've missed some of the fun."

Diarmid stilled. He'd not considered his wager terribly important with regard to Cara, but he also hadn't mentioned it to her. Not deliberately, of course. It simply hadn't come up in the course of conversation. He had no idea what she'd think of it.

"On our way to Dyflin, Finn and I challenged Diarmid to go an entire fortnight without bedding a woman," Dallan explained. "To my knowledge he's managed to do so, somehow."

Perhaps she'd not care at all. It wasn't as though he'd done anything that affected her directly. Diarmid dared a glance her way.

She glared back at him. Diarmid could almost watch as she rebuilt those icy walls, block by frozen block.

Perhaps he'd not be smoothing things over with her after all.

CHAPTER TWENTY-NINE

CARA WAS SELF-AWARE enough to realize that the wager was not a gross indiscretion. She could, quite reasonably, see how it had never been mentioned before. Indeed, logically, it really had naught to do with her.

Cara knew all of these things.

But how she felt was another matter entirely.

Was that why he'd not bedded any women since he met her? Was that why he'd been so interested in her, because he was starved for attention? Was that why he'd then managed to reign in his pursuit of her, so that he wouldn't lose this infantile wager?

Cara didn't want to jump to conclusions. She wanted to speak with Diarmid, to hear the answers to her questions directly from him. When she looked back to the table, the knucklebones were already out, Conan grabbing them to play his trick.

And like that, her patience snapped. Cara couldn't fathom sitting here, playing games, pretending nothing was wrong while she waited to find time alone with Diarmid.

"I'm feeling more tired than usual," she proclaimed, rising from the bench and stepping away from the table. "I'm going to turn in for the night, so that I can rise in time to see you all off in the morn."

Diarmid looked up at her, flashing her a soft smile. "Don't let it bother you if you oversleep," he teased. "I think at least one of us will."

"Someone *always* oversleeps," Dallan agreed.

Conan and Diarmid both burst into laughter. "Says the fellow we had to drag out of his cot to the last battle," Conan said.

"Sleep well," Sitric told her, picking up the knucklebones when Conan set them back down.

Cara passed a good hour or more reading before she sneaked from her room to Diarmid's. She had to wear her hooded cloak, as so many stood between Cara and her destination. Though it meant she needed to hide her appearance, it also meant she'd look more suspicious climbing in his window instead of walking through his door.

She entered the guest hall, her face as deep in her hood as she could manage, and wandered through the press of bodies to Diarmid's door.

To find him waiting for her.

"What are you doing?" she cried, knowing not a soul would hear her over the bawdy songs being butchered outside the door. "Sitric is going to get suspicious if we leave at the same time!"

"Aye, he may," Diarmid agreed, "at which point I'd tell him the truth, as we discussed. But," he added when she opened her mouth to argue, "I've only just left, so it wasn't even close to the same time."

"Still," she muttered, "you're always the last to leave. He'll think it odd."

"I told him his longships were too great a challenge for me," he said, laughing. "What nonsense." Diarmid stood, reaching out to her. "I couldn't wait all night to speak with you."

She took a step backward. "You told me—more than once—that you hadn't bedded any other women since we'd met," Cara began, jumping right to the matter. "Was it because of the wager?"

"I would almost certainly have bedded a maid at the inn when we stayed," he admitted. "But not the innkeeper. I don't steal other men's wives."

Cara narrowed her eyes at him. She wasn't married, but she was well on her way to it.

"You're not married," he defended. "You're not even betrothed. You're intended, which, admittedly, is more attached than I'd prefer, but it is what it is."

"What about after the inn?"

"After the inn, it was entirely because of you." His voice, as thick and sweet as honey, caressed her ears. "In fact, when I explained to Cormac that I found it difficult to stay away from you, he suggested I lose the wager and bed someone, just to keep me preoccupied. I couldn't do it. Couldn't even attempt it. Already I knew it was you that I wanted."

"I believe you," she whispered, though her heart still felt heavier than it ought. "Is that why you wanted me? Because you hadn't—"

"No," he interrupted, as though he couldn't bear to hear her speak it aloud. "That was what Cormac suggested, and what I thought initially, but the more time I spent with you, the more I realized it had nothing to do with the wager—and everything to do with you."

She nodded. Again, she believed him, sensed the truth in his words. But still, she couldn't shake the feeling that she'd lost something. "I have one final question."

"Of course."

"Is that the only reason you've not tried to bed me?" She felt like a foolish girl, not a princess grown, as she uttered the words.

He reached his hands to her again. This time, she took them, letting him pull her into his lap on the edge of the bed. "I tried not to bed you because you weren't mine, firstly. And most recently, because I know that it wasn't a terribly good experience for you in the past and I wanted you to be ready."

"I'm ready," she told him, hoping it was true, hoping this really was as good as it seemed.

Diarmid eyed her skeptically. "Are you certain?"

In response, Cara turned in his arms, pulling his lips to hers as she sat facing him in his lap. They were soft and strong, smooth to the touch yet rough with her own, demanding. Hungry. Cara had missed this closeness with him. She wondered if this wasn't the very reason he'd felt so distant of late. And if, just maybe, this was the way to remedy it.

As their mouths danced, their hands explored. Diarmid, to her astonishment, managed to get her out of her gown without breaking their kiss. Forced to pull away to remove her shift, he took the opportunity to look at her. His hot gaze drank her in as he ran his teasing fingers down her skin, leaving a trail of fire as they tickled her sensitive peaks.

This time, Cara knew, she could finally return the favor. As his fingers reached lower, igniting that now-familiar fire that craved his touch, Cara brushed her hand over the hard cylinder in his trews. He inhaled sharply, a sound that sent desire coursing through her like a rapid. She didn't waste any time relieving him of his clothes in return.

Or grabbing a handful of him and making him groan, stroking him as his fingers plunged into her. When she gasped at the glorious feeling, Diarmid shot her that grin. The one that made everything in her melt for him.

Then he tossed her onto the bed, covering her body with his glorious display of muscles. His hand never stopped massaging her as he positioned himself, slowly easing inside of her, giving her plenty of time to grow accustomed to him.

And it was time she needed. Diarmid was massive. At least, compared with Torna, who was her only comparison. She'd hardly been able to feel a thing other than an erratic rubbing sensation. But with Diarmid, she felt everything as she wrapped around him. Everything.

"How does that feel, princess?" he asked, the gravel in his voice making every muscle in her core clench, his hips working languidly to move him inside of her. His mouth kept busy as well, rendering her incapable of replying at all while he tasted her lips, her neck. While his hands squeezed her chest greedily.

The more they moved together, the heavier his breath grew. Cara felt his chest rising and falling, faster and faster against her own. The fire inside her built to an inferno, demanding to be set free. The ache grew unbearable.

She cried out his name again, this time begging him to release her. He reached between them, his thumb once more circling just above where they were joined until she felt herself falling apart—over and over until Cara lost all sense of time and place. Her awareness returned in time for her to hear his delicious groan as he released himself inside of her.

For long moments afterward, her heart beat so fast and so hard she could feel its steady rhythm against her chest. It had not been terrible at all. It had been incredible.

"So?" he asked once they'd caught their breaths. "How do you feel?"

"Wonderful," Cara whispered. "And tired."

He laughed, a sensual, tempting sound that would have roused her to action were she not so weary. "Sleep," he told her, placing a soft kiss on her forehead and laying down beside her.

Cara had been so uncertain over her relationship with Diarmid. Too much was at stake for her to take this chance and have it fall apart. This time it wasn't only her heart—it was her kingdom, her sister's security, her family's reputation.

After that magical night, however, Cara knew she needed to find a way to make it work. They could speak with Sitric and Brian, come to some sort of solution. And she knew that Diarmid would help her ensure her family didn't lose everything so that she could be with him. He was a good man—the right man, even. And, good Lord, that hadn't been *anything* like her experience with Torna. Diarmid had been right about him. He had no idea how to pleasure a woman. She found herself feeling sorry for whatever poor woman had ended up bonded to him.

Cara went to bed, worrying she'd not make it up in time for dawn. Relief descended when she woke and saw that it was still dark, though the sky had turned a shade brighter near the horizon—dawn was coming. And it would be a day of new beginnings. She turned to wake Diarmid so that he had time to ready himself, and perhaps she'd be able to steal some more kisses. Her hands reached for him, grasping at air. The sheets beside her were cold.

Diarmid was long gone.

CHAPTER THIRTY

DIARMID TOSSED AND turned, sleeping fitfully. He'd grown used to it, over the years. His nerves never bothered him before a battle, but such energy rushed through him at the anticipation of it that he hardly slept at all, even after such a satisfying night with Cara.

He rolled over for the hundredth time, his chest swelling as he listened to Cara's slow, measured breaths. Would she ever grow to love him? He knew now with a certainty that terrified him that he'd fallen irrevocably in love with his princess. But was she even capable of loving him? Or had her heart been broken too badly the last time?

Normally he would go for a walk when he had such troubles resting. Or bed a woman, he mused, but he'd already done that. And the only woman he wanted in his bed was currently fast asleep in it. Pulling the covers up around her shoulders, Diarmid slipped out of bed and dressed in silence.

He brought his sword and dagger with him, as he did anytime he went out alone at night. Dyflin wasn't a dangerous town by any means, but the good folk who lived here weren't the only ones around. Hundreds of men came and went daily from the ships in the harbor. Diarmid believed them good to a man.

He brought his weapons in case he was wrong.

The buxom maid was still tidying the hall when he opened his door. "They're not making you work through the night, are they?" he asked.

She laughed. "No, I couldn't sleep. Too much excitement, I'm afraid."

"You and me both."

Strolling down the wooden logs that lined the sodden roadways, Diarmid inhaled the sharp tang of the sea air at midnight. It had gone cold quickly this year. His hot breath left a trail of white wisps as he wandered the sleeping town. This had been a good decision, clearing his mind before they left in the morn. He could take a brisk walk and get his head on straight, returning to the room before Cara woke.

He still hadn't decided if he had the heart to wake her when he left. Hopefully she'd wake on her own and save him from the matter entirely. Diarmid also couldn't suppress his concern that she so easily doubted him. At every turn, every new development, it seemed that he had to convince her that he hadn't failed her in some way.

The masts of the great sea-faring vessels had just come into view when shouts rang out from further down the road. From The Broken Oar.

Diarmid jogged down the logs, wondering what drunken bastard was itching for a fight before they sailed to battle. He arrived to find Sitric and Conan arguing with a sailor so deep in his cups that even a rope couldn't have saved him had he fallen overboard. That he could stand and converse at all, based on the slur of his speech and lean of his body, was nothing short of miraculous.

Surveying the situation further, Diarmid noted that two of the alehouse's serving women surrounded Maeve, whose dress was torn open straight down the middle. Between the terrified, furious looks on their faces and Conan's death glare—the one he used before *actually* killing someone—Diarmid could surmise what had happened.

Sitric and Conan had the sailor cornered. He wouldn't be getting away without paying for his crimes. But the women, particularly Maeve, actually shook with fear. He approached them slowly, greeting them from a safe distance.

"Are you alright?" he asked, keeping his voice soft, light. "Do you need to see a healer?"

"We got here just in time," Sitric called. "These fine young ladies came to the holding to request aid. Luckily Conan and I had the good sense to stay up all night to finish our *hnefatafl* game."

Diarmid looked at his brother doubtfully. "Conan doesn't even know how to play that game," he chuckled. "How could it possibly take you so long to beat him?"

"Obviously, he taught me to play first." Conan grumbled a colorful curse before turning back to the sailor, who'd stood up and was attempting to charge Conan. His brother's foot connected with the man's chest, sending him back to the ground.

"Go find out what ship he's from," Sitric ordered Conan. "Diarmid and I will mind him."

Conan ran off toward the harbor with a nod, and Diarmid turned back to Maeve. "Are you alright?" he asked again.

She shook her head.

"We need Niamh," Diarmid told Sitric.

"She's not injured, she's shaken," Sitric argued. "Just sit and talk with her."

Diarmid doubted that she'd have any interest in speaking with a man at the moment. "Let's get you inside, and into some fresh clothes."

Maeve led Diarmid through the hall and out the far door. A small, square cottage lay at the back of the property, with a sloped, thatched roof and only one door instead of the standard two. Her companions opened the door for her, revealing a small space where the women no doubt came to get away from the noise and demands of the alehouse.

"I'll stand out here while you help her," Diarmid told them, taking a post in front of the door. "Do any of you know how to fight?"

"No." One of the other women answered. Marga, he thought

her name was, though she'd never been the one serving their ale. "We've never had anything like this happen before. We've never needed to know."

Diarmid wished he weren't on his way out of the town, else he'd stay with them until that ship left. He doubted the sailor would be back, not once Sitric and his captain had spoken with him, but his shipmates might get it into their heads to seek vengeance, however unmerited.

"If a man comes after you, you make sure this," he gestured to his thigh, "comes into contact with this," his groin, "as hard and as repeatedly as necessary to get him onto the ground. Aye?"

The women nodded.

"Then you run for help," he continued. "The beauty of it is that you can be quite close, so if he pulls you in next to him, you can still get away."

"Thank you," Maeve said quietly. "What will happen to him? Will he come back?"

Diarmid crossed his arms, relaxing against the small cottage. "I don't know for certain. It's between Sitric and the ship's captain. But, if it were me, he'd be ship-bound until they sail again and owe the honor price for such a crime. It's possible he'll be banned from sailing here again, though I confess I'm not knowledgeable enough on the laws for the matter."

He also knew that maintaining a good relationship with the captain would be a high priority for Sitric, who was the center of all trade on the island. If it came down to it, Diarmid wagered that Sitric would pay the fine himself to preserve the trade route.

As though materializing from his very thoughts, Sitric himself approached them. "It's all sorted," he announced, handing Maeve a leather pouch. "Here is the payment you're owed according to the laws. He won't be coming back here."

Maeve thanked him, her cheeks aflame.

Diarmid wished them well, stepping away from the cottage to join Sitric. They'd taken two steps before Maeve called out. "Wait! Please," her voice cracked. "Please don't leave us alone."

Fury welled up in Diarmid at the man who'd made her so afraid. "Did you at least get a good hit on the bastard?"

Sitric's jaw tightened. "More than one. He and I spent some quality time together learning manners while we waited for his captain."

Good. "Do you have a father or brother who can come for the night?" Diarmid asked.

"My uncle lives just outside the embankment."

Sitric nodded, his eyes squinting. Diarmid recognized the look—he always wore it when he planned. "Conan, you and I will go with Marga to fetch the uncle. Diarmid, you stay with these two lovely ladies until we return."

Diarmid waited with Maeve and the other woman—whose name he learned was Sorcha—for what seemed hours, though he knew the walk was not so far as that, even across the entire town. He built the women a fire, learned how they'd come to manage an alehouse, and a good deal more by the time Sitric returned with the uncle.

When they stepped out of the cottage, everything finally sorted, pale light played at the edges of the horizon.

Diarmid's gut wrenched. If he didn't hurry, Cara would wake to find him gone.

After he'd bedded her.

Just like the bastard who'd broken her heart.

"I'll meet you at the ships," he called to Sitric, taking off at a sprint back toward his room. The air had begun to let go some of its clinging chill in the face of the rising dawn.

Racing through the wooden palisades and into the guest hall, Diarmid threw open the door to his room.

To find it empty.

CHAPTER THIRTY-ONE

TWO DAYS AT sea did little to calm Diarmid's roiling nerves. Not over the coming battles, nay—over what he knew would be a terrible misunderstanding. Every small obstacle seemed only to widen the growing chasm between them. Diarmid knew that he'd need a ready apology to explain his absence in the morn when he returned from this excursion.

He rowed each day until his shoulders and back burned with the effort, his arms turning to puddles by the time he took his break. Every man on the ship save the captain spent time at an oar.

"They're pulling ahead!" Illadan shouted above the galloping waves and cries of the gulls. "Row!"

Once the men had learned of the wager, *everyone* wanted in. Casting aside thoughts of Cara, Diarmid picked up the pace alongside the other rowers—their final chance to sprint into the lead.

"Row!" Illadan shouted again, standing at the bow and gesturing onward. "We've nearly taken them!"

Row they did. Over and over, pulling against the crush of the water, every oar manned and every man giving his all. When Illadan and the other warriors on their breaks raised a cheer and leaped from the ship, Diarmid knew they'd done it.

Both longships emptied as they rushed the settlement at Cill Cliethe. A small band of warriors were stationed there as protection, but it had never been an attack against men. They'd not come for blood.

They'd come for wealth and hostages.

Brian and Sitric were both at war with the kingdom of Ulaid. Taking men and valuables would weaken them far more than a pointless slaughter.

The aim, of course, was to force them to submit to Brian and acknowledge him as the High King, as well as ending the incursions by Ulaid into his kingdom. Diarmid had long ago tired of the constant fighting between the kingdoms. Having them united under a strong leader would bring a peace no one thought possible—precisely the reason Diarmid stayed with Brian when his father had turned on him.

They charged up the beachfront, seaweed and spume trampled by the feet of nearly two hundred men. The first drops of rain pelted them as they broke through the feeble wooden palisade, built too near the salty seas.

Fighting through the meager force guarding the settlement, the entire raid took less than an hour. By midday, they were hauling chests and hostages onto the third, smaller ship they'd brought for just that purpose. A quick meal later, they left for their second attack: Inis Cumscraigh.

Inis Cumscraigh lay further inland, making it necessary to navigate An Caol, a snaking river that led from the sea to a smattering of inland settlements. More men guarded Inis Cumscraigh than Cill Cliethe, but still nowhere near enough to pose a challenge to them. Once again, they captured what men they could—who would hopefully serve as the leverage in a negotiation—and took all the valuables they could find. If Ulaid had no money for supplies and no men for warriors or workers, the king would have little choice but to swear fealty to Brian instead of inciting more bloodshed.

Diarmid wandered the ruined settlement—one that housed a monastery and, therefore, more of the kingdom's wealth. He joined several of Sitric's men headed into a small dry-stone building, blinking to adjust to the dim light within. Though there was no central hearth, braziers lined the walls of the single room. The cramped interior could only hold two short trestle tables, each with four stools. The room itself was unremarkable.

But what sat upon the tables—spectacular.

A dozen books in varying stages of construction covered nearly all the visible surfaces. Paints, inks, brushes, and an assortment of tools Diarmid couldn't name sat in neat rows down the center of the table, held in cups, bows, and vials. The entire building smelled of books, of dried leather, ink, parchment, and wood.

Cara would love this place.

"Leave them a moment," Diarmid directed the men, who'd begun flipping through the pages. "I'd like a look."

The warriors grumbled, but ceased their rifling, rushing out the door to find other plunder. Diarmid ran his hands down the pages of the first book in the row. It appeared to be an accounting of the events of the past year in their small corner of the earth. It had a few illustrations, but looked entirely too practical. Though, Diarmid thought with a chuckle, some boring record of a village's events may be something his princess would enjoy.

Princess. It had been too long since things had been easy between them. Maybe a gift fit for a royal would be a good first step toward finding that connection again.

He continued down the table, his fingers brushing each item. Diarmid knew that even if they didn't bring all of this back to Dyflin, Cara would want to hear every detail.

"Shopping, are we?" Sitric ducked beneath the low doorway, smiling like a fool. "Looking for anything in particular?"

Diarmid chuckled. "I'll know it when I see it."

"Ah, my favorite kind of shopping."

"Congratulations on your victory," Diarmid said distractedly, his hand moving to the fourth book. It was the most complete, and it had caught his eye the moment he'd begun this exercise—the shimmering paints looked like they'd just finished drying. The magnificent illuminations colored the edges and letters of countless pages. It wasn't a large book, perhaps as wide as a dagger's blade. "This one," he told Sitric. "This is what I'm looking for."

Carefully, reverently, he turned the pages, one after another. And read about Achilles and Patroclus consulting the oracle at Delphi. The beauty of Helen. The great warrior Hector slaying Patroclus, provoking Achilles' anger. The Myrmidons.

Diarmid smiled. Aye, this would be perfect.

Sitric wandered over, looking at the painstakingly illuminated pages. "A good choice." As an afterthought, he added, "I believe Cara reads a lot. Perhaps she'd like to see it."

Diarmid's hands went clammy and cold. This was it. He couldn't drag this out any longer. The battles were won, and soon they'd return and Sitric would expect a betrothal contract.

"I thought to give it to her, actually," he told Sitric. "I believe she enjoys this tale in particular."

Sitric let out an oath. "Do you know her well? You traveled with her, perhaps you've spoken with her more than I have?"

"What do you mean?" Diarmid hadn't a clue. He thought Sitric might intuit his interest in Cara, but his friend seemed relieved—which would be an odd reaction indeed.

"As you're well aware, she's impossible to read," Sitric began, sitting on the nearest stool. "I agreed to the betrothal and she put me off! After practically begging me to agree to it for a fortnight, when I finally do she hesitates. What did I miss?" he asked, clearly baffled. "What happened?"

Diarmid drew in a shaky breath. "I fell in love with her."

CHAPTER THIRTY-TWO

"YOU *WHAT*?" SITRIC rose, a storm rolling over his fair face.

"Entirely by accident, I assure you," Diarmid told him. "We, the Fianna, decided she needed some—help. Learning how to behave more warmly. They asked me to give her some advice, offer some guidance on holding better conversations and the like."

He crossed his arms over his chest, his mail rattling. "Explain it to me," he ordered, his tone measured. "From the beginning."

Diarmid told him everything, trying not to show how much more anxious he grew with each word. Sitric stood motionless, listening. His eyes, fixed on Diarmid, gave nothing away.

"Well," he let out with a heavy breath. "That poses a few difficulties."

"It does," Diarmid agreed. "You have my sincerest apologies. But I imagine that is the cause of her unexpected hesitation." When Sitric didn't reply, Diarmid forged ahead. "I count you among my friends, Sitric, but I understand if this has set a rift between us. I swear, I will make it right."

"Gods, man, it's not as though I'm in love with her," Sitric snorted. "I want her land, her resources. If we can figure a way that I still get them, bed her all you'd like."

"That would be up to Cara and Brian," Diarmid replied.

Sitric nodded. "Aye. I suppose we'll have to start with Cara, then. I'll send a messenger to Brian when we return. He won't come visit himself of course. He's too afraid of seeing my mother," Sitric laughed.

"A truly terrifying woman, indeed," Diarmid joined in. "I'm sorry to have let you down."

Sitric waved a hand. "Think no more of it. Though I wish you'd have told me before I made a fool of suggesting to her that we draw up the contract."

"What will you do next?" Diarmid asked. They'd agreed the decision would lie with Cara, but not upon how to present it to her.

"We let the runes decide," he replied, as though that were the most reasonable solution.

"What? No, Sitric," Diarmid protested.

"I have a plan, never fear," he flashed a grin, though Diarmid would hardly call it reassuring. "We will let the princess choose. If she loves you, she'll choose you. If she won't lose her family's kingdom, she'll choose me. Everyone wins. And once she's made her choice, we can decide on the particulars."

"And how, exactly, do the runes play a part in this?" Diarmid was almost afraid to ask. He walked over to the door, book under his arm.

Sitric leaned in close, wrapping his giant arm about Diarmid and squeezing him into a hug. "I'm glad you asked. It's going to be great—it will be just like in those stories she loves so much. Here's what we'll do..."

CARA HAD MADE a huge mistake. When she sat up in bed the morn the men set sail, it felt as though she'd woken from a fever dream, seeing the world as it was for the first time since she'd met Diarmid.

The world was a disappointment. It was growing close to people only to watch them let you down over and over until you'd had enough.

This morn, as Cara watched the longships approaching the harbor, she'd had enough. Diarmid had left. He'd disappeared after bedding her, not even returning to say farewell. Just like Torna, he'd gotten what he wanted. He'd used all the same words, all the same seductions and games. How she'd missed it, Cara couldn't fathom.

But it mattered not, for she saw it now.

She'd, once again, given him the benefit. She asked after him, to see if one of the maids saw him leave. She had, as it turned out—the one he'd shamelessly pursued at dinner. Cara pieced together information from several folk who'd been up and about when Diarmid left. And every one of them agreed—he'd gone to the alehouse. And folk who lived near the alehouse or who had been there that night all agreed—he'd spent the night with one of the serving women.

Cara hadn't even let herself cry. Such a man wasn't worth a single tear.

And she'd nearly sacrificed her family's future for such a rogue. She shuddered even now as the thought intruded.

The ships made record time into the harbor, and Cara wondered if they'd made yet another wager. She was sick of those as well. The white tips of waves crashed about the smooth wooden hulls, foaming and seething like spirits rising from the grave. Three ships, two pulling ahead of the last.

As they neared the shore where Cara stood waiting, she spotted Sitric at the bow, grasping the dragon's head that reached up from the spine of the ship. He leaped into the shallows before the ship made berth, splashing through the frigid water, and produced his leather rune pouch.

"Fair princess!" he called dramatically. "The runes shall decide our fate!"

Cara hadn't the faintest idea what he was talking about, but she assumed the raids had gone well based on his theatrics. "And what fate is that?" she asked, when he was near enough she needn't shout.

"I hear tell that you love a prince but are to marry a king," he replied. "The runes shall decide who will win your hand."

"But—" she protested, feeling the heat flush her cheeks.

"Ah," Sitric held up a hand. "We let fate decide. What the runes say, we shall obey."

This was madness. Absolute, utter madness.

Cara watched in horror as Sitric tossed the runes, catching them in his hand and reading them.

"I'm curious," he said. "What did your heart want them to say? Who do you wish to wed?"

So that was his game. He used the runes as a ruse to divine her feelings on the matter. Well, Cara knew precisely whom she wished to marry.

From the corner of her vision, she saw the other two boats slam against the dancing shore. She didn't allow herself to look too closely.

"You," she declared, her voice unwavering. "I wish to marry you."

Sitric's brows rose for just a moment, but he quickly returned to his usual expression. He looked down at the runes once more, then back at Cara. "The runes agree."

"Good." Cara's attention moved to the man standing a few paces behind Sitric.

Diarmid.

CHAPTER THIRTY-THREE

DIARMID STOOD, KNEE deep in the rising tide, wondering what he'd just witnessed. For several breaths, he was too stunned to do anything. Then it hit him, harder and sharper than the icy waters roiling at his feet.

She'd chosen Sitric.

What hurt even more was that she'd not hesitated, not paused or considered at all. She hadn't looked for him as he jumped ashore. And when her gaze had finally found him, all he saw was solid ice. A look that froze his heart and then shattered it.

In one look, he knew she wasn't going to give him a chance to explain anything. No matter how many times he proved himself, it would never be enough.

She'd chosen Sitric.

He strode through the thick tangles of seaweed, until he reached her. She watched his every move with that frigid glare. When he reached her, Diarmid thrust the sack he was carrying into her arms, the one he'd filled with a book, wrapped in a strip of leather—as safe as he could keep it from the salty sea.

Then he walked away.

"WHAT JUST HAPPENED?" Cormac sat down across from him at the alehouse, where he'd been drowning his sorrows since he left the harbor.

"I don't want to talk about it," Diarmid grumbled. He knew he owed Cormac an explanation, but he needed time first. He wasn't ready yet.

Cormac politely waved off Maeve when she came to set down an ale for him. "I'm afraid we must." His gaze bored into Diarmid's, forcing him to catch his eye. "Why did Sitric offer to let her marry you?"

"Because I told him I was in love with her." The words forced him to take another swig.

Cormac took away his tankard. "You're going to trip all the way up the hill at this rate."

"Can't think of a better way to get there."

"Diarmid." Cormac's sharp tone sobered him. "Are you telling me that you seriously contemplated letting our mission fail so that you could marry the bride sent from one king to another? To further peace between kingdoms?"

Diarmid blew out a breath, running a hand through his sea-soaked hair. "Well, when you put it that way, it sounds a lot worse."

"That's because it is a lot worse," Cormac grumbled. "I thought you'd changed, brother. I thought you'd finally grown from a child to a man, who stands by his oaths and friends."

He hadn't thought it possible, but Diarmid felt even worse as he listened to his brother speak naught but the truth.

Cormac rose, his lips taut. "I know you're unhappy with the lady's choice," he said under his breath, "but she just did you a favor. If you had actually prevented that marriage, Illadan would've made certain you were no longer counted among the Fianna."

For the first time in his life, Diarmid felt too depressed to drink. Once Cormac was far enough away that he wouldn't risk running into him, Diarmid trudged back down the road toward Sitric's holding, wondering how this day could possibly get any worse.

He didn't have to wonder long.

Before he'd even made it to the guest hall, Cara descended upon him.

"Sitric told me I had to speak with you," she muttered, clearly as excited at the prospect as Diarmid.

He should have kept walking. He was in no state to have this conversation. He should just accept his loss for what it was and start moving on, returning to his old life. "Why?" he asked, his lips betraying him. "Why did you choose him?" His chest ached as he spoke the horrible words aloud.

"Why did you leave?" She turned the question on him so quickly it felt like a slap.

He shrugged. "I couldn't sleep. I took a walk."

"Was it easier to sleep after you bedded the serving maid?"

That got his attention. "What?" he asked, incredulous.

"I asked where you'd gone," Cara told him, fury blazing in her every word. "I was told you spent the night with a woman named Maeve who works at the alehouse. They saw you walking down there. They saw you walk into a building with her."

Of course she would think the worst. She had every other time. Why would this be different? Diarmid realized then that he was tired of fighting to change her opinion of him. If she didn't want to love him, he certainly couldn't make her.

He closed the distance between them, as he used to when he was about to kiss her. But instead of taking her into his arms, he leaned in and whispered his final words to her.

"Always you search for reasons to doubt me, to push me away, to build your walls," Diarmid told her softly. "But it's only an excuse not to let yourself be vulnerable. The problem is not me," he breathed, "though I'm certainly far from perfect. The problem is that you are more worried about being hurt than about being loved."

Her mouth fell open, and he forced himself not to look at those lips. They were his no longer.

They had never really been his at all.

THE STRICKEN LOOK on his face tore at her heart. But he'd left her, Cara reminded herself. For another woman. She ignored the stabbing pain she felt through every part of her body. Ignored the ring of truth his words had held. Ignored the urge to fall right back into his arms.

No, she knew where that path led. Her body may desire it, her heart may ache for it, but her mind knew better.

More irritated than she'd thought possible, Cara spun on her heels back toward the hall. She didn't stop until she sat on her bed, didn't stop even when Sitric and Niamh and Astrid all greeted her. She muttered a feeble reply before disappearing into her chamber.

Why did she still care for a man who'd gone straight from her bed to another woman's? Diarmid's whispered words threaded their way through her mind as she carefully laid the cloth-wrapped book on her bed furs. Cara disregarded them. It couldn't all be some fabrication of her own mind. People had *seen* him.

She'd known the sack held a book by the weight of it, but she'd not had time to open it until now. With gentle hands, she peeled back the leather strip, a small piece of parchment, torn and tattered, lay atop the book.

For my princess.

Scribbled in what could only be Diarmid's writing, by the messy, uneven strokes. Cara swore an oath. Why did the man have to be so charming? He wasn't even here and he was winning her over, making her question what should be a simple decision.

If it were so simple, Cara wondered, then why did she still wonder at all?

CHAPTER THIRTY-FOUR

SHE READ THE entire damned book that night. Devoured the illuminated pages as she saw the story she so loved brought to life before her eyes. Achilles' hair shimmered gold, the shields and armor a brilliant bronze. When she looked at the deep blue of the water as the Greek ships sailed to Troy, she could almost feel it lapping at her skin, the warm sun on her face. Every character could be found somewhere within those magical pages.

When she read, Cara disappeared. She forgot all about betrothals and marriages and princes and kings—*her* princes and kings, anyway. It was just her and the story.

So when she turned the final page, closing the cover with a sigh, disappointment crept through her at the prospect of returning to her actual life. Yet, it must be done. She stood, placing the book back in its wrappings and storing it safely in the chest by her bed, her heart aching as she thought of the man who'd gifted it to her.

Directly following the morning meal, Cara, Sitric, Illadan, Cormac, Broccan, and Gormla met in the great hall, sitting at one end of a long trestle table. Illadan, Cormac, and Broccan represented Brian in the contract; Gormla sat in to aid Sitric. For the first time since he'd left on the raid, Diarmid's absence was palpable, following her even when he was nowhere to be found.

She wondered what would have happened, had she chosen him. Would they have sat here today, she and Diarmid and all the rest of them, negotiating some alternate contract? Would they have needed to send word to Brian first? Whatever they discussed, she knew Diarmid would be grinning at her. Just like he always had.

She was being ridiculous, she reminded herself again.

"Cara?" Cormac's voice intruded on her outrageous stream of thoughts.

Lord, she'd missed the entire conversation. "Excuse me," she said, "I'm afraid I didn't sleep well." Or at all. "Could you repeat that?"

"Could you give us a minute, please?" Sitric asked, rising and offering his hand to Cara. "We'll be back before you miss us," he told the others with an easy smile.

They stepped out of the hall into a blistering eastern wind, a harbinger of the coming storm. Cara considered asking if she could return for a cloak when Sitric stepped into one of the smaller halls further back on the property. Built in the same style as the two larger ones, but a quarter of their size and with only one door.

"These are for various purposes," Sitric explained, holding the door for her and closing it tightly behind them. "When we have guests like Brian, especially if he travels with his wife, we offer these cottages for their use. Or, as we are doing, I use them for private meetings when I don't want anyone in the hall listening in."

"Is something the matter?" Cara asked, unable to decipher Sitric's unusual behavior. Granted, she found a good deal of his behavior unusual, but pulling her from such an important meeting and taking leisure time to speak in a cottage felt especially odd.

Sitric moved about the room, lighting the four braziers that stood, one in each corner. "You tell me."

"Do you mean my misstep at the meeting?" she asked. "I really did get very little sleep. I'm terribly sorry that I wasn't paying attention."

"Don't be," he replied, his manner so easy she could forget he was a king. "It was so tedious it nearly put *me* to sleep," he teased. "Why did you get so little sleep?"

Cara rolled her lips, considering whether or not to tell him the truth. "I was reading," she admitted sheepishly.

"The book Diarmid brought you?"

She nodded.

"Did you enjoy it?"

"Very much," she replied honestly. "If you don't mind my asking, why are we here? I'm certain it's not to talk about my irresponsible reading habits."

Sitric chuckled, taking a seat on the bed—a near duplicate of the one in her room. "In an odd sort of way, it is, actually."

What in the world did that mean? Cara inclined her head questioningly.

"When was the last time you stayed up all night reading a book?"

Cara thought a moment. "Honestly, I can't recall. It must have been while I was still a child, having just learned my letters."

"Precisely," Sitric told her. "You are responsible to a fault, to my thinking. I could sense it when we met, and it was one of the things that made me believe we would not be a good match."

"Are you saying that you like me more now because I stayed up too late?" Cara couldn't scrape together a direction from any of his random questions.

"Hear me out," he pleaded, his voice quiet, insistent. "If you never do this, why now? Why last night? What kept you reading?"

"I was enjoying the story," Cara answered, feeling that much was obvious.

"You've read it a hundred times. It couldn't only be that."

Cara hesitated. "And, it kept me from worrying about…everything else."

"Aha!" Sitric stood, now pacing the small room with his hands behind his back, as though solving the world's greatest mystery. "My final question," he promised. "What thoughts were distracting you so at the discussion just now? Your honest answer, Cara."

The way he said it, Cara could tell he already had his suspicions. So she gave him her honest answer. "Diarmid," she whispered, her chest filling with guilt.

"Don't worry yourself over injuring my feelings. I like you," he said, his deep voice filled with kindness, "but I never loved you. I simply thought that one day I could."

"Did Diarmid put you up to this?"

"No," Sitric chuckled. "He wished me well in my marriage and apologized for the four hundredth time for romancing my future wife. If he tries to apologize again, I may actually punch him, but not for the transgression. Just to end the interminable apologizing."

"I appreciate your understanding and kindness through this mess that we've made," Cara told him, "but I'm certain I've made the right choice."

"You stay up all night reading the book he brought you to keep yourself from thinking about him. Then, when you're forced to do anything else, you can't stop thinking about him long enough to have a conversation that will determine your future. I'm not so certain you did make the right choice, and I felt obligated to point it out before this went too far."

Cara couldn't possibly change her mind now, even if she wanted to. Which she didn't. "What of the runes?" she challenged, knowing how he trusted them. "They agreed with me."

Sitric flashed her a grin that put her in mind of Diarmid. Again. "They didn't, actually."

"What?"

"I planned to go along with whatever you said," Sitric admitted. "But the way they fell, they very clearly told me you should marry Diarmid. And, I must say, I'm inclined to believe them."

CHAPTER THIRTY-FIVE

"ANOTHER ROUND FOR my friend!" Dallan called, waving Maeve over and slapping Diarmid on the back.

Diarmid didn't want another round. He didn't really want much of anything. Except Cara, and even that he wasn't certain about any longer. "Do you think we drink too much?" he asked no one in particular.

"Good God." Conan nearly choked on his ale. "Alright, first, you know they water it down, right? It's like we need to drink two cups to actually have one. And second, aren't you the one who claims there's no point to life if you don't enjoy it?"

"It's possible to enjoy things other than drinking," Diarmid tried, wondering which of his friends would disagree first.

To his surprise, it was Finn, whom he'd always considered the most reasonable of the bunch aside from their fearless leaders. "It's not possible to drink less while being hosted by an Ostman," he said. He didn't even sound like he jested. "My father always said drinking with a man is the best way to get his measure."

"That, actually, explains a lot about Sitric," Dallan replied, furrowing his brows as his dulled wits contemplated the idea. "At least you won the wager," he added, his voice too cheery.

"That's true!" Finn jumped on that small victory. "You don't even have to pay for these drinks."

"I didn't actually."

This time, Conan actually did spit out his drink. "What was that?"

"I went thirteen days," he told them, desperately trying to keep the memories of Cara from intruding. "Not fourteen."

Dallan swore an oath. "Truly?" his incredulous voice would've been fodder for teasing if the topic were different.

Only Finn didn't look surprised.

"Does Sitric know?" Conan's brows furrowed.

Diarmid did take a drink then. "He does."

Silence descended as his three companions looked at one another. Diarmid couldn't bear to see their faces, knowing he'd failed them as well.

He'd failed everyone, it seemed, though at least he hadn't completely ruined their mission in the end. When none of them spoke, Diarmid couldn't take it any longer. "I'm sorry I failed you," he said, not meeting their gazes.

Every single one of them reached for him, Finn and Conan leaning across the table to give his shoulders an affectionate shake. "Don't say that," Conan ordered. "You're a rogue and a drunkard, but I won't let you lie. You did no such thing."

"He's right," Dallan agreed. "Everything worked out in the end."

Except it hadn't.

Cara was marrying Sitric instead of Diarmid. She wouldn't even have a civil conversation with him, believing that he left to bed another woman that night. Even if he had refuted it, she'd not have believed him.

Cormac hadn't spoken with him since yesterday, at this same table. He'd finally been getting to know his eldest brother, the one who'd always been so different from him. Diarmid had managed to destroy that bridge before he'd even finished building it.

They were right, he supposed, that at least the mission had succeeded. When they arrived in Dyflin, Diarmid believed the only commitment he was capable of making was the oath he'd sworn to Brian, his oath into the Fianna.

As he sat listening to his friends try their hardest to cheer him, laughing and joking and celebrating their victory at The Broken Oar, Diarmid determined there was one other commitment he was prepared to make—a marriage to Cara.

With no hope of such an outcome before him, Diarmid supposed he'd have to make do with a successful mission for the Fianna. Though, at this point, he wouldn't hesitate to exchange one for the other.

CARA SAT IN the coziest chair in the seating area in front of her room, a warm woolen blanket draped over her and *The History of the Trojan War* cracked open in her lap. Astrid and Gormla had gone to the market in town, searching for silks that wouldn't cost enough to give Sitric palpitations. The Fianna, apparently having enjoyed their adventure aboard the Ostman longships, hurried down to the harbor at daybreak to continue training, Sitric with them.

After speaking with Sitric yesterday, they'd returned to complete the betrothal at her behest. As per Brian's wishes, when she married Sitric, he would become king of Thurles, her sister remaining as steward in Sitric's absence. The kingdom, meager though it may be, would remain in their family, giving both Cara and her sister security after the debacle with Aodh and giving Sitric a position within Brian's kingdom and a smattering of more fertile lands.

She should be thrilled to have achieved all that she'd hoped for and to have recovered some small part of herself along the way. Try though she may to be proud of her accomplishments, Cara felt wretched.

The door to Niamh's room opened beside her, giving Cara a start. "You're up late," Cara commented, furrowing her brow. "Are you feeling alright?"

"Oh, aye," Niamh replied gently, shutting her door behind

her. "I stayed up too late last night."

Cara nodded, looking back to the beautiful book in her lap. "I'm familiar with that problem."

Niamh let out a soft laugh, grabbing herself a blanket on her way to the chair across from Cara. "I've not read that one all the way through," she commented, pulling her legs up under her and draping the blanket over her lap. "Do fewer people die at the end than at the beginning?"

"More, actually," Cara said.

"My father spent a fortune on a tutor. He was not terribly pleased when he learned I hadn't finished all my reading."

"I didn't realize you were a noble." Cara mentally chided herself for never having asked after Niamh's family before. The woman had been tending her own family's aches and pains for years. Cara realized then how little she knew about someone she'd lived beside for six years.

"Oh, I'm not," Niamh replied hastily. "My father is a merchant."

Cara wondered at that. She knew the healer lived in a cottage with her mother and maid—which, she realized belatedly, explained why Niamh and her mother *had* a lady's maid. But she'd never heard of a father. And Niamh spoke as though he yet lived. "What happened to him?"

Niamh's lips tightened. "I wouldn't know," she said. "He left."

"I'm so sorry," Cara told her. "I'm sure you were devastated—I cannot imagine it." She'd fallen apart when Torna had left, and he'd been in her life but briefly. Cara couldn't begin to fathom what she'd be like now if it had been her own father who left.

"Thank you." Niamh wrapped her arms about her knees, which remained tucked tightly beneath her brown woolen blanket. "It made trusting people difficult," she said, her voice oddly tentative. "With Dallan, for example, I was so afraid that he would leave me and break my heart that I left him before he had the chance."

Ah. So that's what she was getting after. Cara sighed, growing weary of everyone else giving her advice on Diarmid. "I'm glad that it worked out for you and Dallan," she replied, "but I don't see how it could for me. My family's kingdom isn't worth spending my life with a man who hurried to bed the first serving maid he could find."

Niamh's eyes narrowed. "Do you mean Maeve?"

"I do." Cara's chest tightened at the thought. "Everyone saw him there with her."

"That's what you believe happened? That he went down to the alehouse and bedded her?" Niamh shot out of her chair, laying the blanket over it and reaching for Cara. "Let's go."

Cara bristled at the unexpected command, but closed her book and stood, sensing Niamh wouldn't relent until she cooperated. Moving far more leisurely than Niamh, Cara folded her blanket and walked her book back to the storage chest in her room.

"Where are we going?" she asked as Niamh strode toward the door.

"To the alehouse."

CHAPTER THIRTY-SIX

CARA HELD BACK her protests as she and Niamh went down the now-familiar split-log road into the heart of Dyflin. Though she felt this exercise entirely unnecessary, Cara knew that Niamh wouldn't drag her all this way, to see this woman in the flesh, for no reason. Niamh was nothing if not kindhearted. So Cara kept her fretting to herself.

It was the first time Cara had actually been to the alehouse in Dyflin, though she'd heard more about it than any sane person could take. The men frequented it, finding it an entertaining change of scenery from Sitric's grand halls. Even Sitric himself enjoyed the place.

"Niamh!" A petite, brown-haired woman rushed to embrace the smiling wisewoman. "Can I get you a drink?"

"Actually, I need a favor, if you can manage it."

"For you, anything." The woman hadn't hesitated even a moment before giving her vehement response. "I could never repay you for what you've done."

"Maeve, I'd like to introduce you to Cara," Niamh said, gesturing in her direction. "If you feel up to it, I need her to hear about what happened that night. From you."

Maeve paled, but nodded, wiping her hands on her creamy apron. "You mean with Diarmid and Sitric?"

Cara's stomach dropped at the casual mention of his name. But what of Sitric? Had he been here as well? No one had told her that.

"Precisely so," Niamh encouraged her. "If it's too difficult for you—"

Maeve waved her hands. "No, no. As I said, if it's of help to you, then I'm happy to do it. Best come back this way, though."

They followed Maeve into the alehouse, a thatched roof hall supported by wattle and daub walls, much like every other Ostman homestead she'd seen. She walked through it to a cottage, much like the one Sitric had taken her into, and stopped just in front of the door.

"What would you like to know?" Maeve asked Cara.

"Tell us what happened, from the beginning until the men left in the morn," Niamh answered for her.

"A group of sailors came down to the alehouse first," Maeve began slowly, clearly recalling the night as she spoke. "Marga and Sorcha—the women who work here with me," she explained, looking at Cara, "they'd gone to take a break as hardly anyone was in, what with the big feast up at the hall. They drank as sailors usually do, getting rowdier and deeper into their cups than I like to see. They all stood to return to their ship for the night, but one called that he'd be there in just a moment." Maeve's voice shook at her last words.

Niamh grabbed Maeve's hand, in both of hers. "If you need to stop, we understand."

"No," Maeve whispered. "It's best to get it out, not keep it in, as you always remind me." She turned her attention to Cara. "He attacked me. Tore at my clothes, started wrestling me to the ground. The girls, when they heard me screaming, they came out of the cottage and bolted straight for Sitric. None of us could do a damn thing.

"I'll spare you the details, but Sitric arrived just in time, Conan right behind him." She smiled then. "That was the first time I heard a bone crack, when the two of them went after him. You can imagine it caused quite a commotion, though the neighbors all poked their heads out of their houses without coming to see the truth of it or offer aid. Diarmid, though, he'd been out walking and he came running. He said he'd heard a raucous at the alehouse when I asked him later.

"Anyway, Sitric minded the sailor while Conan went to find the ship's captain. Diarmid came to the cottage to stand guard in case any of the man's shipmates came back for him and started a brawl. By the time they'd gone and fetched my uncle to stay with us after that, they all had to rush back to get to the harbor by dawn."

Maeve took several deep breaths as her story came to a halt.

Cara looked to Niamh, who nodded, her beautiful face looking like an angel of vengeance, ready to go find that sailor and break another of his bones. "Thank you," Cara told Maeve, her own voice now shaking. "I know that wasn't easy for you to share."

"If you see them, will you thank them again for me?"

"Of course." Cara's mind reeled as she processed Maeve's tale. Why hadn't Diarmid told her that?

Because she wouldn't have believed him. He'd said as much, and she knew deep in her bones he'd been right. And she'd been very, very wrong.

Cara had a mind to stay and get to know Maeve, but several customers seated themselves and she had to rush off to get them their ale. Cara satisfied herself with a promise that they'd both come back to visit Maeve. Not only did Cara's heart break over this woman's horrifying experience, but she owed Maeve more than the woman knew.

By sharing the worst day of her life, Maeve had stopped Cara from making the biggest mistake of hers.

"Why are you helping me?" Cara asked Niamh while they meandered down the rows of thatched roofs and wattle fences. "Doesn't Dallan want me to marry Sitric since that's what Brian commanded?"

Niamh clasped her hands behind her back. "Aye. But I'm not Dallan." She threw a mischievous grin at Cara, quite uncharacteristic of the mild-mannered healer. Or, more likely, perhaps Cara didn't really know Niamh at all. "And, as I said in the hall, I don't understand what you're going through with Diarmid, but I do understand the fear of being left behind."

"I was so certain," Cara sighed, weary of weighing her decision over and over. "But this changes everything."

"Have you considered why it is that Diarmid is the person you felt safe enough to work with?" Niamh asked, waving to a gaggle of children who were smiling at the pair of them. "Why couldn't it have been Sitric, or even me, who helped you?"

"It was always easy with him," Cara admitted. "I trusted him."

"You still do. You let him in right up until you realized that he'd gotten close enough to really hurt you, and then you pushed him away. Having pulled such a ploy myself once or twice, I'm quite familiar with the symptoms."

"What made you decide to change?"

"I pushed him away hard enough that he really left. It took less than a day for me to realize I'd rather have my heart broken a thousand more times than live another day without him."

Of all the things anyone had said to her over the past sennight, Niamh's words were the ones that truly helped Cara see the situation clearly.

She'd done nothing but war with herself over her decision to marry Sitric since the moment she agreed to the betrothal. She'd found every way to distract herself, she'd pushed Diarmid as far from her as possible, to the point where he hadn't felt comfortable trying to explain himself to her.

Because he shouldn't have had to.

Her heart had known all along what her mind refused to acknowledge—that Diarmid was a man worth taking a risk on. Hopefully, it wasn't too late to show him just that.

CHAPTER THIRTY-SEVEN

DIARMID WOKE AT dawn, opening his door into the guest hall to find everyone else with their heads together at one of the four long trestle tables down the large center aisle. The moment his door shut, every last one of them looked at him.

Diarmid crossed his arms, raising a brow. "Well? Are you plotting my murder, then?"

Conan scoffed. "Do you think we'd be so obvious about it?"

"Yes," Diarmid shot back. "Though I'm flattered you feel it would take—" he counted the people around the table, "eleven people to do me in."

Cara was missing, he noted, the ache in his chest that had become a constant companion bloomed once more. He wished she were there, that he could see her. He wished to never see her again for the turmoil it wrought within him. More than either, Diarmid wished for an end to this wretched misery that followed him about. Hopefully it was but a temporary affliction.

"Are we not training today?" Diarmid asked, walking over to the table to join them. "Are we leaving?"

"We were debating that very thing," Illadan answered.

Niamh frowned, looking up at Diarmid pleadingly. "I left my satchel in the guest cottage," she groaned. "Diarmid, would you mind fetching it for me before you sit with us?"

Diarmid sensed some sort of ploy. "If there's a man waiting in there to kill me, you're burying him," he told her.

"Thank you!" she called after him as he headed for the little cottage behind the halls.

At least this morn was interesting, if nothing else, he decided. Diarmid reached the little thatched-roof building in no time, since it sat only a few paces across the green. Throwing open the doors, he knew to expect *something*. This was, after all, nothing if not a contrived errand.

But he'd not expected to find Cara.

Sitting up on her knees on the fur-covered bed.

Completely naked.

Diarmid shut the door so fast he worried the walls might crack. He didn't turn around to face her, instead leaning his with his arms against the door. There was no way he'd be able to have any kind of a conversation while she sat like that. Just a glimpse of her and he fought to control his lust.

"I owe you several apologies, it would seem," she began. "I'm sorry that I thought the worst of you, when you continue to believe in the best in me. I'm sorry if I made you feel unloved or unwanted. And most importantly, I'm sorry that I chose Sitric at the harbor that day."

"What of him?" Diarmid asked, looking down and back, but not so far that he could see her. "You signed the contract, did you not?"

"He burned it."

Diarmid did turn then. "But what of Brian?" He took a step toward her. "What of your kingdom, Sitric's new lands?" What of her? Had she truly changed her mind?

"If you accept my proposal, Illadan, Finn, and Cormac will return to Brian with a message from Sitric requesting alternate choices for his bride and explaining that Sitric and I were not a compatible match."

He didn't hear most of what she'd said, his heart had stopped after her first words. "If I do what?"

"If you accept my proposal," she repeated. "Of marriage."

Finally, he allowed himself to take a long, lingering look at her, his whole body growing hard. "I thought you wanted to slow things down."

"I was scared," she whispered, "because I realized that I love you."

Diarmid sucked in a shaky breath, taking another step toward her. "Say it again."

"I love you."

"Well," Diarmid grinned at her, the ache in his chest finally easing, "then maybe we should get married."

The corners of her lips turned up until her mouth arched into the sweetest smile he'd ever seen. A real smile.

Diarmid took the last steps to the bed, climbing right on top of her and lowering her onto her back. "You have the most beautiful smile."

"I'm working on bringing it back," she said.

"I'll savor each and every smile I get." He planted a soft kiss on her lips, loving the way it felt to be with her again.

"I brought games," she whispered, her voice husky. "And wine." Her hands pushed off his trews as she lay beneath him, freeing him and taking him in hand. "I am prepared to make some *very* bad decisions today."

Diarmid swore an oath as she worked him, her eyes dancing with mischief every time he groaned. He felt the pressure at the base of his spine, threading its way up, craving her body on his. "I need to be inside you, princess," he managed, unsure how his voice was still functioning.

She smiled at him again, a sight that he would never tire of seeing, and reached for the knucklebones. "You're going to have to earn it," she teased, handing them to him.

He took them, still unable to believe that this strong, remarkable princess sat beside him.

And that, finally, she was all his.

CHAPTER THIRTY-EIGHT

DIARMID, CORMAC, FINN, and Illadan rode hard out of Dyflin the following day, heading for Brian's fortress at Caiseal. Diarmid had spent the entire day in that cabin with Cara. An entire, incredible day. It had been nothing short of a gift, and he would always treasure it as such. He'd helped her improve her skills at knucklebones through powerful motivation, a learning method that had proved both fun and effective.

When they stopped to water their horses and take a small meal of waybread and salted pork, Diarmid went out of his way to catch Cormac alone. He'd made amends with Sitric. He was en route to make amends with Brian, hoping this wouldn't cost him his place among the Fianna. But Cormac had hardly spoken a word to him since they'd sat together at The Broken Oar. And after having his brother in his life, Diarmid refused to give up on him.

"You'll have to speak to me eventually," he said, handing Cormac a waterskin. "I'd prefer it was sooner rather than later, if it's all the same to you."

His brother's dark look told Diarmid a humorous approach was not the way to go. "I'm sorry that I let you down," Diarmid tried again, this time aiming for honesty. "I should have told you before I spoke with Sitric. I shouldn't have risked the mission. I knew you'd be disappointed in me again, and I was enjoying getting to spend time with the version of you who didn't see me as a failure."

Cormac considered his brother, drinking deeply from the waterskin and handing it back to Diarmid. "I was trying to show you that you could trust me," Cormac replied reluctantly. "It hurt when it was clear you still couldn't."

Diarmid placed a hand on his arm. "I'm sorry," he repeated, not looking away from Cormac. "I was doing much the same myself," he admitted with a smile.

"Shall we try again?" Cormac asked.

Diarmid grinned at him. "Absolutely. Let's start with you telling me what's going on with you and Astrid?"

"I already told you," Cormac growled. "She's the devil's mistress, sent here to torment me."

Diarmid barely contained a snort of laughter at his eldest brother. Never in his life had Cormac said something so outrageous, especially about some poor, innocent woman. He stopped prodding him for now, but he could not wait to see what happened next with *that*.

They rode for three days, the weather a miserable sheet of rain for much of it. When they reached Caiseal, Dunla, Brian's wife and Diarmid's eldest sibling—a full four years older than Cormac—rushed out to greet them. She hugged Diarmid and Cormac, greeting Finn and Illadan and ushering them all to the hall.

Brian's feasting hall was an immense, round building, constructed in the style of the ancient kings of Éire. Much like Sitric's hall, it had a central hearth and seating scattered about. The Fianna followed the queen into the hall to find Brian seated by the hearth. Diarmid noted that more often than not, as the king aged it was the spot he favored. Brian, still a tall man though his hair had long since greyed, stood to greet them.

"What news?" he asked, his shrewd eyes taking in the men before him.

Diarmid stepped forward. "It's rather a long story," he began. Then he proceeded to tell the entire course of events to Brian, who listened without a hint at his thinking. When Diarmid finished, he explained that Cara had offered to gift Sitric a portion of her lands in recompense for the broken engagement, and so that he might have access to better resources for his kingdom.

"I'm beginning to wonder if Finn Mac Cumhail required his Fianna to marry for love as a test to his own patience," Brian muttered, bringing a hand to his impressive grey beard.

Diarmid apologized again, not knowing what else to do as his king deliberated his fate.

"The oath was clear," Brian began, "the Fianna must marry for love. If you love her, I must allow it. Cara will remain queen of Thurles, but Sitric will be king by law, not marriage, and entitled to one half of the resources from those lands. I realize it is an unusual solution," Brian said, "but it's also quite an unusual problem. I will consult with my advisors before I send you back."

"Back?" Cormac asked, sounding horrified. "You mean to deliver the news to Sitric and return with the princess?"

"Oh, no, you'll be in Dyflin a good long while yet, if my instincts are correct. Sitric won't be getting away without a wife, though I'm certain he'd hoped as much."

Illadan raised a brow. "Do you have someone else in mind?"

Brian flashed them a devious smile. "Two someones, in fact. And you'll be staying until he's wedded and bedded one or both. I don't care. Just get him married." He turned to Dunla, who sat quietly embroidering beside them. "Wives are one of life's great joys," he declared. "And it's time Sitric takes one."

A SENNIGHT LATER, the Fianna returned, their numbers twice what they'd been when they set out from Dyflin. Brian had chosen two women, who'd each brought a lady's maid, to present to Sitric. As much as Diarmid wanted to watch Sitric's reaction to Brian's new orders, he couldn't take his eyes off Cara.

Before he'd met her, he would have laughed at the notion that he'd fall in love and be betrothed to a woman in less than one turning of the moon. That he'd happily and willingly bed only one woman for the rest of his life. The moment the reception had ended and the new guests were taken away to see their rooms, Diarmid lifted his princess into his arms.

He kissed her until she gasped for breath.

And the smile she gave him as he carried her into their cottage told him this was only the beginning.

About the Author

Sophia has been telling stories since she could talk. She loves learning almost as much as she loves writing, pursuing both her undergraduate and master's degrees. She has studied archaeology, anthropology, and the languages and histories of a variety of cultures. Her master's degree is in medieval history, with a focus on the British Isles. She's been fortunate enough to participate in three archaeological excavations and surveys–one at a Native American settlement in southern Indiana, one at a Tudor estate in Essex, and one at an early medieval ringfort in County Roscommon, Ireland.

After marrying her high school sweetheart, attending grad school, and moving nearly ten times in as many years, Sophia and her husband settled into a lake house in northern Indiana. When she isn't working on her next novel, you can find her in the garden and covered in dirt. They live happily in the middle of nowhere with two little boys, two atrociously rude doggos, and one ornery cat.

Facebook:
facebook.com/SophiaNyeWrites

Instagram:
instagram.com/sophianyewrites

TikTok:
tiktok.com/@sophianyewrites

BookBub:
bookbub.com/authors/sophia-nye

Goodreads:
goodreads.com/author/show/20815931.Sophia_Nye

Amazon Author Page:
amazon.com/Sophia-Nye/e/B08L9XZ148

Website:
sophianyewrites.com

Milton Keynes UK
Ingram Content Group UK Ltd.
UKHW020858110624
443837UK00013B/350

9 781963 585667